T H E I R
WILD
ISLAND

Paul Bolster

Copyright © 2025 by Paul Bolster

Maudlin Pond Press values and supports copyright. Copyright fuels creativity, encourages diverse voices, promotes free speech, and creates a vibrant culture. Thank you for buying an authorized edition of this book and for complying with copyright laws by not reproducing, scanning, or distributing any part of it in any form without permission. You are supporting writers and allowing Maudlin Pond Press to continue to publish books for every reader. Please note that no part of this book may be used or reproduced in any manner for the purpose of training artificial intelligence technology or systems.

Original Illustrations: Paul Buechele
Front Cover Painting: Elizaveta Kalacheva
Back Cover Painting: Lillian Bolster
Author Photo: Nathan Bolster

ISBN: 978-1-959563-40-2

Maudlin Pond Press
P.O. Box 53
Tybee Island, GA 31328
www.maudlinpond.com

Printed in the United States of America

*To Dr. Fred Marland
and the young scientists to follow*

Jack

Chapter 1

I yanked my suitcase out of Mom's car and rolled it toward the water. Stepping onto my grandfather's dock, I could see the green shoots of spring peeking through the bright yellow of winter cordgrass. A small creek bordered the Tybee Island cottage where Mom grew up. An artist would love this scene. That is not me. The small motorboat was what interested me. The *Mary Joe II* wasn't the big tour boat Papa Joe once owned, but I could see it did have a fifteen-horsepower motor. For me, growing up in Atlanta, any boat with a motor got my attention. *I wonder how fast it can go. I hope we'll spend some time on it,* I thought. *I'd love to take it over some sick waves.* The boat strained at its moorings as the incoming tidal water moved swiftly up the creek. The marsh, the water, and the boat might make a small improvement in this spring break. But a week with Papa Joe?

Maybe I can survive if I can get my mind off what my friends are doing. That thought pushed me back into the start of the day. With my mom driving, we swept past the Atlanta suburbs a little after the sun came up and arrived on the island just before noon. Five hours of watching the boring Georgia landscape was not a good beginning for my spring break. As soon as we were on the road, Mom got deep into conversation with her legal assistant about the big-deal real estate transaction coming next week, and I put in my AirPods and clicked into my K-pop playlist. I loved the lyrics, but the music didn't dampen my anger about the trip. My mind flashed back to the confrontation.

"Why, Mom? Why do I have to spend my whole spring break week with Papa Joe? The last time I was on Tybee Island was when Grandma Mary died. I was only nine. Papa Joe didn't pay any attention to me. He was just so sad."

"I expect that he is still sad and lonely, but a visit from you might change that. Maybe you could take some of his sadness away and brighten him up a bit. And it's time you get to know your grandfather. He grew up on Tybee, and I'm sure he can show you parts of the island you've never seen before."

"Just what I need. Someone to lecture me some more, teach me stuff I can read online or in books. On spring break, you chill out with your friends and forget about school. This grandfather thing is not cool. I can see the smirks on my friends' faces when I go back to school with old dude stories."

"Jack, you agreed to a family vacation, and Papa Joe is about all the family you have left, at least on my side."

"Okay, Mom, I agreed to a family vacation, but that was when you and Dad were going to come too, so we could have 'together time' or whatever. Now it's just me and some old dude who hasn't seen me in four years."

Mom didn't answer, so I pushed a bit more. "It's not my fault you and Dad bailed because you were 'too busy.'"

"Why not Hilton Head with Devon, or Seaside with Chris and Jim?"

"Listen, Jack," her irritation rising *"your dad and I try to do what's best for you."*

"I know what's best for me."

After a moment of calm, she tried a different tac-

tic. *"Covid is not done with us, so a big gathering of out-of-control teenagers at the beach is off the list. And maybe you need a little space from your friends. And from your computer and your smartphone too."*

"Wait a minute!" Now my anger surfaced, and I went into full battle mode. *"You're not going to send me off to some island and cut me off from contact with all civilization. No way, Mom!"* I had to think quickly to strike a bargain. *"While I'm away, you're going to want to talk to me, right? Besides, you try living a whole week without your cellphone. I'll do it if you do it too."*

"Okay, okay," she sighed. *"I guess if I want to be able to get in touch, you need to have your phone, and you might as well have your laptop. Maybe you can write something. An email or two on how you're doing would be nice."*

"Mom, no one uses email."

On the trip I didn't give an inch. *She started this.* We stopped in Macon at Mom's favorite barbecue place. "Do you remember this?" she asked.

"No," I muttered. I gave her no satisfaction.

Privately I thought lunch was killer, but when we got back on the road, Mom's phone buzzed, and the endless discussion of documents to limit liability started again. *What a hypocrite*, I thought to myself. And then, the truer, sadder thought emerged: I could disappear from this car, and she wouldn't even notice.

On the five-hour trip from Atlanta we stayed in our own corners. Neither one of us was giving an inch, but we also didn't want to take up new battle stations.

* * * * *

I sat down on the dock and let my feet dangle inches from the cool water of the incoming tide. I looked down at my phone and scrolled through the posts on Instagram. There it was. My friends were already hanging out on the square at Seaside. *It's not fair. I always seem to be on the outside. Maybe I'm better with everyone online than in person,* I began second-guessing myself.

At school when I mentioned to Jim and Chris that Covid made me feel cut off from the rest of the world, their only response had been "Real." No back and forth. But when I'd texted Devon to ask what courses he'd be signing up for next semester, we went back and forth for half an hour, discussing which teachers were best and which classes gave too much homework.

For sure life had improved after lock-down. I went to Shaky Knees with my bros and listened to the sickest music. I can't imagine me and Papa Joe going to a concert on Tybee or in Savannah. I'm gonna be bored, bored, and bored with my slow-moving grandpa for a week. A whole week on Tybee.

Just before my mood hit rock bottom again, Mom yelled from the back deck. "Papa Joe's on his way home from a late breakfast with his buddies. He'll be here any moment. Bring your suitcase up to the house. I'm sure you'll have the upstairs to yourself."

Papa Joe

Chapter 2

I poured my first cup of coffee and sat at the kitchen table opposite the empty chair. Mary's chair for forty-five years. She had helped me get started every day of my adult life. Her advice had kept me balanced and sane. I was alone now – and lonely without her. What advice would she give me now?

"Choose joy." She said it every day.

For me, that was harder and harder to do. At age seventy, I realized the names of people and places I'd known my whole life sometimes escaped my memory. I was still out of bed before the sun, even before that old alarm clock jangled. I still went through my exercise routine, but my day-to-day activities were becoming less interesting. It was harder to find anything exciting.

"Choose joy," I murmured to myself. *Maybe today will bring some with that grandson of mine,* I thought. *But what do I know about today's teenagers? Can my world and his connect?*

I glanced again at Mary's chair, and I could almost hear her say, "Just be yourself. Get to know what's important to the boy. Think about what you wanted from your Uncle Ben when you were thirteen. And for Pete's sake, don't ask him what he's studying in science class or what he wants to be when he grows up. Respond to what he says."

Carrying my coffee mug, I walked out onto the dock. The back of the house faced a small tidal creek,

and I loved it when the early morning sun touched the browned marsh. Since the dock looked west, toward Savannah, the sun took some time to hit the creek's still waters. But when it did, the brown marsh popped bright yellow as if daubed by an artist's paintbrush, contrasting with the deep-blue waters of the tide-filled creek.

These were my moments of pure delight. Maybe, just maybe, I can help Jack feel a little of this too.

* * * * * *

I handed Mildred a twenty when I checked out of the Breakfast Club. "Keep the change, Mildred." I knew the change was getting smaller over the many years she'd waited on me and my friends. Everyone around me was aging. She was part of the Tybee institution known as The Breakfast Club, where I rendezvoused with my two oldest friends. We checked in regularly with each other, and since I lost Mary, we spent more time together.

"How you doing today?" asked Mildred.

"I'm good. More than good. Thanks for asking."

"You seem to have a little spring in your step, and you're the first to leave your regular gathering. Something special happening today?"

"I didn't know it showed. My daughter, Sharon, and her son Jack are going to arrive from Atlanta in a few minutes. He's staying for a week while she hustles back to her busy life. I'm really looking forward to knowing him but still a little worried about how to entertain a thirteen-year- old city kid."

"You're going to do just fine," assured Mildred. "This place will entertain him. I'm sure Jack will find a way. Your dock is one of the best fishing spots on the island."

"Not sure about fishing. Hard for a teen to wait for the fish to cooperate. I think city kids may need something moving fast."

Joe felt a little guilty about rushing away from his friends. He'd known Billy Wagner and Willard Elliot since they were kids. Billy had a thirty-year career as an enforcement officer for the Georgia Department of Natural Resources (DNR) and Willard was an environmental scientist with a PhD from the University of Georgia. Together, they knew all there was to know about the marshlands and the coast of Georgia, and if they didn't know the answer to a question, they knew someone who knew someone who did know.

As I walked toward home, I laughed to myself about Willard's suggestion at breakfast. Willard, who served on the local Planning Commission, followed closely the environmental issues which threaten our coastal way of life. He suggested Jack could come to a meeting of the commission and hear a young female scientist explain the Tybee plan to counter sea level rise. Now, I love Willard and his scientific mind, but I also know that mind is far removed from the mind of a thirteen-year-old.

I'm sure Jack gets most of his education over his laptop. He does that well, but what kind of life is that for a teenage boy? I shook my head. At Jack's age, Willard, Billy, and I had made our own private map of the local islands, and Uncle Ben taught us the ways of the animals, the fish, the shrimp, and the tides. *On what map would my city grandson and I find common ground?*

Again, I could hear Mary talking to me, "Listen to Jack."

Jack

Chapter 3

Mom had only one evening on Tybee, so Papa Joe suggested A-J's Restaurant, just a ten-minute walk from his place. I remembered that from A-J's dock on a large curve of the Back River you could see the forested uplands and marshes of Little Tybee Island. The Taylor family had celebrated many milestones at A-J's.

"You probably don't remember, Jack, but we came here for Grandma Mary's sixty-fifth birthday. You were just eight, though," Papa Joe said.

"Wow! This is the perfect time to be here," Mom enthused. "I love to see those skimmers patrolling the edge of the beach. Look, Jack," she urged. "They're hoping to snag small fish. See how their beaks are extended and sharp on the bottom?" I rolled my eyes even though I thought it might be pretty cool to see those birds grab a fish.

Papa Joe added to her comment. "If you keep your eyes peeled, you might see a dolphin or two. They're active in the river when the tide is ebbing. They swim against the flow so they can catch the smaller fish coming out of the marsh. The dolphins are at the top of the food chain, and they feed on what the marsh produces. They also brought customers to my tour boat,"

Here we go, I thought. *I guess parents don't stop teaching even when their kids are grown up. I can see where Papa Joe is going with this nature stuff. He wants Mom to move back here. Well, I'm not getting sucked in.*

Luckily, Mom was quick to head off the tour-guide lecture. "You know I know that, Dad. I got an A on my ninth-grade paper on that exact subject."

"Well, Jack probably hasn't read it."

I sat quietly, not responding. I was listening, but I wasn't going to let on. I was just glad their attention turned away from me. Mom hastened to fill the silence.

"How are you doing, Dad?" she asked.

"I'm good," Papa Joe said brightly. "I'd rather not be old, but as they say, it's better than the alternative."

"No, really, Dad."

"Every day I take a bunch of pills that are supposed to prevent bad things from happening. The doctors haven't found anything that's going to kill me anytime soon."

"That's not what I mean," Mom persisted.

But Papa Joe wouldn't let her below the surface. He was probably a little like me. Didn't want to be mothered and knew where this conversation could go. "I'm pretty fit for an old man," Papa Joe replied. "I get my 7,000 steps a day." I could see the quick wave of loneliness cross his face as he thought about rattling around in his empty house. That gave me a moment of pause, thinking what it must be like for Papa Joe.

Mom gave up, "Good! I'm glad we'll have you a while longer. You might even be in better shape than I am. I don't get much muscle tone from sitting at my desk and punching keys."

"What happened to all that athletic prowess you showed when you lived in this little town?"

"I was in a tennis league for a while, but you know how stuff always comes up at the law firm. When a partner needs something done, you have to get on it."

Yeah, I thought, *the law firm comes first... and second... and third.*

Papa Joe was a little alarmed. "Are you getting any exercise at all?

"We have a Peloton in the basement," Mom continued sheepishly, "but I have to confess it's been a while since I've been on it." Trying to shift the conversation, she turned to me, asking, "What do you remember about our visits to Tybee?"

They're not going to leave me alone, I thought. *I might as well jump into the water.*

"I remember the giant sandcastles we made," I began. "Ours were the tallest because you'd bring a real shovel, Papa Joe, not one of those cheap plastic jobs. And I loved body-surfing. You could always go farther than me, Papa Joe, but I'll bet I can beat you now."

"We'll see about that," he said, gladly accepting the challenge. "Do you have a favorite beach critter?"

"The sand dollar. Remember the time we found hundreds out on the sand bars off the end of the island? It was right after a storm. I had a big bucketful. I bleached them with Clorox and sold them to a Tybee tourist shop for fifty cents each. That was great! My friends couldn't believe I came back home with real money."

"Oh, no," Papa Joe grimaced. "Keep your voice down in case there are any environmentalists around. Now they have signs at all the beach entrances saying to leave the sand dollars alone or throw them back in the water unless they're already bleached by the sun. They're not endangered, but..."

"Endangered environmentalists?"

"Well," Papa Joe chuckled, "I see you've got the Taylor family sense of humor."

"Should we order some food?" Mom broke in. "I'm having my fried oysters!"

"I'll have a hamburger," I declared, knowing I was

challenging mom, and gave the look all Taylors have in their arsenal

"No," she quickly responded to the bait. "You order seafood at a seafood restaurant."

Papa Joe hurried to avoid a confrontation. "I'm planning to grill hamburgers on the back deck tomorrow night."

"All right," I said grudgingly. "I'll try the shrimp and grits. But don't expect me to love it."

The food came. I disappeared into my own thoughts. Mom talked to fill the silence. *There she goes*, I thought. *More about her wonderful life in Atlanta.* Instead, I turned my focus to the folk singer on a little stage in the corner, who wasn't half bad, though his stuff was old. I would've preferred indie. But listening to folk was better than listening to Mom go on and on about deals and lawyers and restaurants. I was too loyal to disagree with her description of her exciting Atlanta life. And I certainly wasn't in a sharing mood about my own. I couldn't see any spots where my life fit into the stories of the other two generations.

Papa Joe

Chapter 4

As usual, I was up before the sun and had coffee waiting when Sharon came into the kitchen, pulling her bag. "I see it's an early start back to Atlanta."

"Yes, this client is a big developer, and it's the first time the partners have put me in charge. The investors are putting up millions, and they want all the risks covered. If I do well on this one, the next deal might come right to me."

"I hope you know I'm a very proud father. I don't know much about development, but I do know lawyers have to pull all the pieces together. Your mother would be very proud too."

"You don't need to know about my business, Dad," Sharon said lightly, "but you do need to come visit us in Atlanta. We have a big house now. And our neighborhood is so sweet and safe. In some ways, it reminds me of the streets around here. Lots of people walking dogs and pushing baby carriages."

"Sounds perfect," I assured her, but privately resolved to stay right where I am.

"How are you really doing, Pops?" Sharon asked.

"Well, in the words of Garth Brooks, 'I got friends in low places.'"

"What does that mean?"

"Billy Wagner, Willard Elliot, and I keep tabs on each other. You know there's always something going on in local politics. I've been reading a lot more, too. It's one of the wonderful habits I picked up from Mary.

She always brought the hot new mysteries home from the library, and she started that book club. It's still going strong."

"So, what are you reading?"

"Oh, mysteries, mostly. And some U.S. war history. This Ukrainian thing, the Israeli/Hamas war, and the whole Middle East conflict has brought back my soldiering memories."

"Didn't Mom also get you into poetry?"

"She used to read me a poem every day, and I'd get caught up in her excitement. A few lines from Dylan Thomas have stuck with me. 'Do not go gentle into that good night. / Old age should burn and rave at close of day; / Rage, rage against the dying of the light.' I'm going to rage as long as I can."

Sharon smiled, showing me all was well and she understood. "I'm glad you aren't going anywhere, gently or otherwise. Our future does seem pretty dark at times, but I hope you and Jack aren't going to sit around and watch the news all day. What *are* the two of you going to do this week?"

"Do you have any ideas for us? Maybe something you did as a kid?

"I couldn't tell you what," Sharon replied with a rueful shrug. "I seem to have tunnel vision these days."

"No problem. I've got a plan. We'll do what Jack wants to do as long as it includes me. I hope he's not expecting me to wear headsets and listen to Atlanta hip-hop or techno music," I chuckled. "My marching orders for the week are to listen and find joy. Those orders come directly from Mary."

"Mom always had the right approach, didn't she?" Sharon said wistfully. "I'm hoping Jack connects to this place and to you. It'll be good for him to spend time away from some of his Atlanta friends. All they do is sit in front of a screen playing video games.

Sometimes they play together, sometimes he plays on-line with random people. Maybe he'll show you how, but don't be surprised if it's way over your skill level. I couldn't get it."

"Is there some problem with his friends?"

"I don't think so. The problem is, for nearly two years he's had to distance himself from other kids his age, and now they're thrown back together. There've been a few fights at school. His counselor told us the kids have been shoving down their feelings for so long that now the feelings are erupting."

"The experts I listen to say some kids didn't do so well with screen learning and they've fallen behind," I said, a little worried. "I can see how that could create some bad feelings."

Sharon took a breath and plunged on. "I'm afraid Jack lost that time, and it's hard to get it back. He doesn't say much about conflicts at school, but I think he got close to some of his gaming buddies on social media during the pandemic, and now that everyone is back at school, those friends are going in different directions. Maybe he feels a little deserted. So now he has the challenge of making new friends."

"Maybe Jack will talk about things this week. Don't worry. I'm going to be a good listener," I assured her. "I was once thirteen. I had some great friends back then. We had adventures together, and we talked some about serious stuff too. Sometimes I didn't make the smartest choices, which led to adventures you don't even know about."

"I can only imagine," Sharon grinned. "Jack's a lot like you. He loves trying new things." With that, she placed her coffee cup in the sink. "Now I have to put the pedal down and run back to my other life," she said. "See you in a week."

"In a week," I answered. After a quick hug, I took

my second cup of coffee and strolled out to the back deck, remembering adventures on my island and enjoying the lure of the waking marsh.

Chapter 5

I slid the screen door open, went out of the house and sat beside Papa Joe on the dock.

"You sleep okay?" he asked.

"Yeah," I replied. "It's really quiet here. I heard Mom leave at the crack of dawn. I'm sorry I missed her, but it's not that unusual," I shrugged, looking down at my Air Jordans.

"I can scare up some breakfast," Papa Joe suggested, "but first, maybe we ought to get a plan for today. I'm sure you know most of what visitors do here: museum, beach, sandcastles, and lighthouse. What floats your boat?"

I looked up quickly. "The boat," I replied with enthusiasm. "I remember riding in your big tour boat through the thin marsh rivers and riding over some big waves. I'd like to get out on the water in that one tied up at your dock."

"Great! I was hoping you would!" I could see Papa Joe was elated. "I've trimmed and gassed her up, and the weather looks all right. No storms on the horizon. This isn't the big *Mary Joe* cruiser. When she started up, those twin 90-horsepower Johnsons would rattle your back teeth. This is just an 18-foot johnboat. Wide beam, flat bottom. Perfect for shallow marshland, but not good on the ocean when the wind is whipping up the waves."

"But how fast will she go?" I wanted to know.

"She's only got a 15-horsepower Yamaha, but at

full throttle she'll flatten out and hit thirty. She's great for fishing and crabbing and putzing around in the marsh creeks. She'll pull a light person like you out of the water on water skis - although not with the power you'd really like. I think it might work. I still have Sharon's slalom skis, and I do know some folks with bigger engines if you wanna do a faster ride or jump some waves off the beach."

"I've never water skied, but I'd love to try," I said, a bubble of enthusiasm rising in my brain despite my efforts to contain it. "Maybe another day. Right now, I think I'd like to get in the marsh and see what's on Little Tybee."

I could tell from Papa Joe's broad smile I had given the right answer. "We'll have to check the tide. Everything here is connected to the tide cycle. The *Mary Joe II* keeps some water under her in the big marsh streams even at low tide but not in the little creeks when the tide is half out. I don't know if you remember this, but the tide matters more here than at most beaches. If we time it right, we can use one of the marsh creeks to get to the backside of Little Tybee Island."

I checked my phone for the tide charts. I liked showing Papa Joe how useful my phone was. "High tide is at 1:30," I declared. "And it's only 9:30 now. How long do we have to wait?"

"We should be able to get through Jack's Cut by 11:30 and for two hours on the other side of high tide," Papa Joe answered as if reading my mind. "That'll get us to the deeper water of the Tybee Slough on the back side of the Island. The Cut is a narrow winding creek that connects the deep-water Back River to the open water of the Tybee Slough. From there we could go up the Intracoastal Waterway, out into the Savannah River and all the way to the big city."

He paused and then with a grin added, "I'm not sure why it is called 'Jack's Cut,' but you can claim it."

Jack's Cut. I thought to myself. *That sounds cool.* I liked the idea of having something permanent—or even not so permanent—with my name on it. *You pretty much have to go through the Cut to get into the marsh. I'm the Gatekeeper.*

"What do you like for breakfast?" Papa Joe asked. "I have cereal and milk, or we can go big with bacon, eggs, and hash browns. Do you cook?"

"No cooking skills," I admitted. "Just mac and cheese from a box and ramen noodles. But cereal is fine for me." I wanted to get going. "What do we need to bring with us?"

"Hmm," Papa Joe mused. "Let's take a couple of crab traps. And probably some rods and the tackle box in case we get inspired. And some binoculars. Oh, and bring your phone. It's good to be able to communicate from out there, and you may see a few critters crying out for a photo."

My excitement began to mount. "I'll be all over that!" I exclaimed, patting the phone securely in my jeans. "One of my favorite things at school has been photography club. Maybe I can catch some video." *I'll send it to the guys,* I thought, *show them Tybee is just as dope as Hilton Head."* To Papa Joe, I said only, "I'll go get dressed."

"Probably long pants, and long sleeves," Papa Joe advised. "We'll need some bug spray too." Glancing at my feet, clad in flip-flops this morning, he added, "Those aren't going to work in the marsh, and I'm sure you don't want marsh mud on your Jordans. Look in the shed for some marsh boots in case we want to get out on an oyster reef or slog through the marsh. No bare feet in the marsh grass or on an oyster reef. Those oyster shells cut like a razor."

"Don't forget a hat!" he called after me. "That spring sun is hotter than you think."

"I didn't bring a hat."

"Look on the rack in the hall. There's an old Vietnam Vet ball cap hanging there."

"It's okay to wear that?"

"I think people will know you're not the vet, and a proud veteran let you use it," Papa Joe assured me.

I'd read about World War II and had passed by the Veteran's Hospital outside of Decatur. Once Mom mentioned that Papa Joe had gone to Vietnam, where his leg had been injured, but that was all she'd said. I'd seen the scar on Papa Joe's calf. *Why is it that veterans don't seem to want to talk about actually being in war? I wondered.*

Chapter 6

By eleven o'clock we were motoring down the tidal creek, past A-J's, across the Back River, looking for the marsh river opening just north of the largest Little Tybee upland.

To reach Jack's Cut, boaters have to get into the deep marsh river that drains a large section of the north end of Little Tybee marsh. They also have to know it's there. Sand bars at the opening move regularly, but I knew where to look. A channel is always kept open by the out-flowing tides. Massive amounts of water go in and out twice each day. Beyond the entrance, the deep river snakes for half a mile through the cordgrass.

Vegetation blocked the view on both sides of our boat. "This is so cool," Jack declared. "Where did all the houses go? All I can see is the marsh grass."

I called his attention back to the water. "Watch the small fish breaking the surface. It means bigger fish are prowling under the surface. Here there's always enough water at low tide for bigger fish to hunt. I've even seen dolphins here."

In the distance the island's bright yellow beach tapered south for nearly a mile, and its thin maritime forest spine narrowed to a point where the tide flowed out of the marsh's southern end. Behind the small barrier island, the marsh spawned many small hummocks protruding over waving marsh grass.

"The larger hummocks have built up over the

years from dead cordgrass and vegetation that manages to live above the tide. These hummocks are great places to camp and spend the day with a fishing rod or a cast net," I explained.

The marsh grass was just beginning to green up from its winter brown and stretched west almost as far as the eye could see. No signs of urban life to the west. The expansive area dwarfed the upland of Tybee Island.

"Keep your eye out for dolphins. There are more than 300 in our part of the coast, according to the DNR."

Jack strained his eyes, hoping to be the first to sight a rising fin.

"Here's where Jack's Cut begins," I explained. "It may not be deep enough for us to get through yet, so let's take a little time and break off some oysters from this reef."

"Wait, Papa Joe!" Jack was alarmed. "Isn't it dangerous to pull oysters from just anywhere?"

"It's okay," I assured him. "My friend Billy Wagner has tested the water right here and found it almost bacteria free. No cesspools adjoining this marsh river. You do have to be careful, though. Oysters are bivalves, and they get nutrients by filtering the water. If there's bacteria, they sometimes collect it, and the direct sun multiplies it. But if you pick the ones below the water for most of the tide cycle, you're pretty safe."

Jack joined me in putting on heavy rubber gloves. Then we leaned over the side of the boat and reached down under the water to break off chunks of oysters. We looked carefully for the fat ones, pushed them into a mesh bag, and threw the loose empty shells back on the reef to keep the bank of the creek from eroding. New oysters need to attach to old shells in order to grow. We stored our harvest on ice in a large plastic can.

I guided the small boat through the ten-foot-wide snaking stream until we emerged on a wide expanse of water. I twisted the Yamaha's throttle to full and sped south. There was a high-pitched whine from the motor, and the wind tore at our loose clothing. Jack looked up, and I noticed the grin on his face matched my own. After a mile or so, we slowed as the Tybee Slough ran close to the tree-lined island and the opening to the ocean. We pulled up as near as we could to the shore, out of the way of passing boats.

"This used to be good place for these crab traps," I directed. "Put some of those old chicken bones inside, and make sure the buoys are tied nice and tight. We'll leave them here for a couple of days and see what happens."

After we dropped the traps into the water, I brought the boat into a little marsh stream that ran along the backside of the island. "I camped here with my friends when I was your age. This time of year is good for camping, but you want a good onshore breeze in the summer. The no-see-ums can drive you nuts."

"What's a no-see-um?"

"A tiny insect you can only see when it bites you," I said, heading the boat towards shore.

"Let's tie up here at the campsite where there are no ocean waves. This was our favorite spot when my good buddies Willard and Billy and I were exploring this island. Great fishing here, and we had an easy walk to the beach on the other side of the island. We had that beach all to ourselves."

We walked under the sprawling live oak which shaded a flat spot for a tent.

"Look Papa Joe, someone has built a little shelf with a nice flat top. It'll probably help getting meals ready if we camped here."

I didn't share his enthusiasm. I frowned and let out a little groan.

"What's wrong?"

"Someone's built a little structure here."

"What's wrong with that?" Jack asked. "It looks like it might make it easier to set up a camp. It's a place to store your food off the ground."

"Well, you know I'm an old timer, and I was taught to live by the rule: take out what you bring into a wild place. This is a little thing, but it's hard to stop people when they start building stuff out here. The State of Georgia owns all the hummocks, marsh, and the bigger upland island. The DNR has designated this whole area a Heritage Preserve. We're free to come here, but we're not supposed to change it."

"I can see that," he answered thoughtfully. "Do you think we could find out who's doing the building?"

"Maybe, but for now let's leave that to DNR's enforcement officers. It can be a little touchy to call people out. Let's walk around to the beach side of the island and hope we don't see more developed campsites. Not many visitors get over here, and I bet we can find some interesting shells."

Jack was amazed. We couldn't see another soul on the long stretch of white sand. *Where were the crowds?* he wondered. You could see homes on urban Tybee just minutes across the inlet, but nothing was visible looking south or north. "This place looks wild," Jack whispered. "It's kind of like being Robinson Crusoe on a desert island."

We found two large undamaged whelk shells and some horseshoe crab shells. Lots of oyster and clam shells. One huge cockle shell that was still hinged. Off the beach, puffy white shorebirds paced a sliver of sand where the waves were breaking. When our stomachs began to grumble, we sat down on the quiet beach to share peanut butter-and-jelly sandwiches and a sliced apple.

After a long, still silence, Jack asked, "Is it okay if I take a selfie with you? My friends have got to see this."

"Sure," I replied nonchalantly, hiding a smile of pride.

Jack aimed his phone north, up the long beach, with a close-up shot of the two of us in the foreground. As he touched the camera button, he glimpsed some movement in the background, at the water's edge. A large bird.

"What's that, Papa Joe?"

I turned quickly to see. "Wow! That's America's bird, a Bald Eagle! It's unusual for them to come so close to humans. There are two nests somewhere here on Little Tybee. I'm sure he or she is looking for food. There's probably a hungry juvenile waiting in a nest. Don't move. Let's see what it's after."

A small tern was limping rather badly away just a few hops from the eagle. As we watched, the eagle attacked the ailing bird with talons and beak. It was not an even contest. Shortly, the eagle was flying away over the trees, the dead tern in its grasp.

"Wow," Jack breathed, suddenly remembering to exhale. "That was brutal."

"It's the wild part of nature," I stated matter-of-factly. "The strong live off the weak. The large live off the small and slow. There is no court of justice or any moral ideal protecting the weak from the strong. No punishment for taking what you need to survive. But see how majestic that predator is, and think of the offspring going to get fed. The parents won't kill more than they need to survive."

Jack thought about that for a moment. "Maybe humans should take only what they need."

"We do have laws that discourage us from taking advantage of the weak," I said, "but that doesn't seem to stop people from taking way more than they need, especially around here. Development keeps eating up the places these wild creatures need to survive. Even the people camping here are taking little nibbles."

"Can we find the nest to see if these eagles have young ones?"

"We'll try a little later if you like. I think I know where to look."

"Papa Joe, how is it that all this beautiful area has stayed so clean and natural? I'd think it would be filled with big fancy houses and big boats and signs saying, 'Private Property, Keep Out.'"

"Well, that's an interesting story," I said, ducking my head a bit. "I'm proud of the part my friends and I played in the fight to keep Little Tybee the way it is today. There's a short version of the story and a long version. Which one would you like?"

I braced for my grandson to ask for the short version. But Jack surprised me. "Since we have almost a whole week together, let's do the long version," he said. "Maybe in small chunks." I think he was a little leery about encouraging adult lectures, but maybe he could tolerate a story or two. After all, he asked the question.

"With pleasure," I replied. "Let's get started. "It was my big teenage adventure with my best buds, Willard Elliot and Billy Wagner. And it started almost on this exact spot. We often camped right where you and I tied up the boat." Sensing Jack's keen interest, I continued.

"All three of us had grown up around boats, camping, and fishing. Our mothers trusted us to be out here as long as we had the short-wave radio tuned to the Coast Guard station. No cell phones back then," I grinned. "The radio operator had my mom's number and would report on our progress. Sometimes, if we had enough money for supplies, we'd camp for the whole weekend, and even longer during school breaks. Didn't need much food. We caught fish and crabs and learned how to get oysters to pop open by putting them near the fire."

"So, what was the big adventure that started here?" Jack pressed.

* * * * *

Papa Joe's Story

Early one morning we saw some men come up the beach. They had surveying equipment and a big machine that looked like a drill. Willard was a talker and would talk to anyone. Willard wasn't afraid of nothin', so he walked right up to those men.

"What you doing on this island so early in the morning?" he demanded of the man closest to him, a short, round guy with a cigar stub crunched between his teeth.

"I could ask you the same," the man grunted.

"Oh, we're just camping," Willard said, introducing me and Billy. "We live on Tybee."

"Well, we're just surveyin'," the man answered with a shrug.

Willard was persistent. "What y'all surveyin'?"

"The tree line, the high-tide line, the elevation, and we plan to find out what's under them trees," responded Round Man, pointing to the drilling equipment. Then he chomped down harder on his cigar.

I told him the tide line was hard to find and it

changed with the moon. "Somebody asked you to find the line? Maybe we can help and earn a few bucks for gas and bait," I offered.

Round Man wanted to end the conversation. "Look, Sonny," he began. Boy, we hated being called 'Sonny.' "We've got work to do here, and you boys need to run along and get on with whatever you're doing. We don't need no help."

Rude! As we gave him an annoyed look, Round Man changed his tactic, "Hey, do your parents know you're out here on someone else's land?"

That lit a little fire in all of us. We turned back toward the campsite and moved away from Round Man. "This is *our* island," Billy muttered defiantly. He was usually soft-spoken, but now he was riled. "What they think they're going to do out here?"

"They're gonna do something big," Willard said. "That was expensive equipment they're carrying around. Did you see? It said Whitaker Construction Company, Atlanta, Georgia. I don't like big Atlanta business creeps poking around here. I bet it's not our interests they're looking after."

Before we headed home that day, we paddled our boat up the marsh stream that runs along the back side of the island until we reached the midpoint. Carefully, we crawled through the marine forest to a place where we could see 'em and hear 'em quite well. I'm pretty sure they couldn't see us. Those men were driving stakes into the ground just beyond the tide line.

"They're marking off lots," whispered Billy. "I think they're seein' how many big houses they can squeeze onto this island."

We crept back to our boat and paddled to our campsite before we fired up the noisy Johnson outboard.

* * * * *

Jack

Chapter 7

Time had slipped away. "Well, maybe that's enough of the story for now," suggested Papa Joe. "We can fish another day. I don't want us to miss the tide window through the Cut. Maybe you'd like to run the boat on the way back?"

Eyes wide, I answered enthusiastically, "I've never done that!"

"I was doing it on my own when I was your age. It's about time you learned. Every island adventurer needs to know how to get home."

I sat at the stern and followed Papa Joe's directions. I put the motor in neutral and pulled the starter cord. It didn't start on the first two weak pulls. "Hey, that takes some doing," I puffed, a little out of breath.

"You're going to have to do better than that to get her started."

On the next pull I leaned back for leverage and was rewarded. Using the reverse gear, I moved the boat into the open water of the Slough, then shifted to the forward position. Slowly I opened the throttle and smiled broadly as the boat made its way north toward the Cut. I edged up the throttle and soon we were moving swiftly across the calm water.

"Slow her down," Papa Joe yelled over the noise of the motor, pointing to something in the water. "Straight ahead. About 100 feet. I think we have our first dolphin sighting."

I slowed the boat too quickly, and a little water came over the stern. Then I shifted into neutral, and the boat drifted to a full stop. When I looked up, I could see a six-inch fin coming straight at us. Papa Joe, balanced carefully in the bow, had his binoculars aimed at the fin so he could see any special markings. He saw more than that. A heavy polymer fishing line wrapped around the fin.

"Jack, get your phone out. Maybe we can do some good here. I want you to take a picture of the fin when our friend comes up for a breath–as close as you can get."

I was quick with my phone. "Will it hit the boat?"

"No. It can see us close up and knows where we are from far away."

When the dolphin came up for air just 20 feet from the boat, I snapped a zoomed-in image which showed a commercial fishing line that might be cutting into the front of the fin.

"Let's turn around and see if we can get a little closer for another picture of the fin. Let me take the outboard tiller and you man the camera," Papa Joe instructed. We switched places. The dolphin was headed south, and we slowly caught up and stayed alongside for a few minutes.

The boat didn't seem to bother the dolphin, and I got three good shots of the fin at close range and shot a short video as the dolphin went under. "Videos give more context of what's going on than a picture," I told Papa Joe.

The photography done, we turned back north. As Papa Joe made a quick dash for the Cut, he said, "I want you to do one more thing." He called out Billy Wagner's cell number and asked me to send the photos with the text: "Is this a problem?"

"Billy still keeps in touch with his old DNR buddies and will know who needs to see your pictures and decide if this dolphin is in any danger. It looked like the line was already cutting in," Papa Joe explained. "They probably know exactly who this dolphin is by the unique markings on the fin. The DNR biologists keep a searchable file on lots of the dolphins in this part of the marsh."

"Is that like face ID?"

"Maybe so," he replied. "But you likely know more about that than I do."

The transfer of the photo was a piece of cake for me. I felt like I was born with a smartphone in my hand.

"Sometimes a snag may not be important, but other times it can be life threatening. We're doing the right thing reporting," Papa Joe said.

Reporting duties done, we switched places, so I could take us home. With only a little help from Papa Joe, I made a few turns off the Slough and found the narrow entrance to the Cut. I slowed the boat to just above idle.

Just before we entered the creek, Papa Joe suggested, "Shift to neutral and listen."

It was quiet at first, and then a couple of clicks came from inside the deep marsh grass. When the boat hit the edge of the nearby oyster reef there were more clicks. I looked questioningly at him.

"It's a covey of Clapper Rails," he explained. "Sometimes they're called Marsh Hens because they're a little over a foot long and look like skinny hens. I've only seen them a few times."

"I hear them, but I can't see anything. Where do they live?" I asked.

"Most of the time they're walking on the mud surface and sliding their skinny bodies between the grass looking for fiddler crabs, snails, and worms they can catch with their long beaks. When they're getting ready to have little ones, they build a nest high enough on the cordgrass to keep the eggs out of the tidal water and away from predators."

"They're well hidden," I admitted. "But they sure make a lot of noise. It's cool knowing they're wandering about."

I shifted the motor into gear and at the lowest speed began to move through the creek that connected us to the deep marsh river, then the Back River, and finally home. The water level was now two feet below the base of the grass stalks, and the creek was getting shallower. In one place with a 180-degree-turn-back curve, I miscalculated and ran the boat up the mud bank.

"Not a problem," assured Papa Joe, "slip it into reverse and she should come right off. Just be gentle so we don't end up in the other bank. I'll push us off with the oar if needed."

It worked. Before we started forward, I handed my phone to Papa Joe. "Would you mind shooting a video for me? I want my friends to see me running the boat through this snaking creek."

"OK, I'll try, but I've never made a video before."

"It's all set" I assured him. "Tap the round red button at the bottom of the screen. Just touch it once and when I've made a couple of turns, touch it again to stop. A quick shot is all they need to see."

"Well, that was easy," marveled Papa Joe as he

carefully handed back the phone.

I thought about how good it felt to show something new to him.

I kept to the inside of the S-turns for the rest of the narrow winding stream. We came back at the right time. The mud banks now appeared on both sides of the narrow creek. In another fifteen minutes, the motor's propeller would be churning up mud or worse, mired in the bottom mud.

When we were out of the winding Cut, the marsh river widened and deepened. I stopped for a minute to review the video. "It's perfect. You got some nice angles in there too. You can feel the tilt of the boat as it rounded the turns. You're a pro! My friends are gonna love this."

Then I watched the tidal flow carefully. Ripples on the surface meant a sand bar just under the surface. The sand bars at the edge of the Back River could stop you. I found the channel without help. On the final stretch to Papa Joe's place, I opened her up to full throttle. "*How cool is this!*" I thought, as I carefully pulled alongside the dock.

With a broad grin, I declared, "Papa Joe, that was a great day! I can't believe we were that close to a dolphin! What was he, about eight feet long? Thanks for letting me drive the boat—it was awesome!

"I love that island and its marsh and everything in it," I enthused, "I almost feel like it's also <u>my</u> island now. I'd like to get down in the mud and see the life it's got, and I want to know more about how you saved it."

"Well, I'm warning you again, it's a long story," Papa Joe said with visible pleasure. "Maybe later. Right now we boatmen have to clean the boat and get some dinner started. You may also want to give your mother a call," he added.

"Probably not today. I need to build up to that," I said quickly, thinking, *I care about Mom, and want to share with her, but I don't want to hear her telling me to be careful, not to drive too fast, not to tire Papa Joe out by doing too much, and whatever else she might think to warn me about. I want to use my own judgment and make my own decisions for once. I think Papa Joe will keep me from making too many mistakes.*

Papa Joe said he usually put the chunks of oysters in a hot oven to pop the shells open. But tonight we were having hamburgers on the grill, so when the coals were red hot he added some of the oysters.

"Put an oven mitt on, and when you see one pop open, grab it off the grill," he demonstrated. "Take a flat dull dinner knife and force it into the crack, like this. Pry the top shell off. Voila! There's a beautiful raw oyster!"

"Yuck," I grimaced. "Looks like a giant booger."

"Put some sauce on it and chew it a little," Papa Joe instructed. "Then let it slide down your throat. It's more about the feeling than the taste."

"It's hard work getting these slimy things out, and I'm not sure they're worth it," I muttered to myself.

"Papa Joe, it's very cool we picked these right out of the ocean, and I suppose if you catch something, you ought to eat it, but... I'll try ONE, and maybe it'll grow on me."

Dinner finished and everything put away, we sat together on the dock. The outgoing tide had drained the creek. The sun was ready to disappear, but neither one of us was ready to let the day end.

"Maybe it's time for a little more story?" I suggested.

* * * * *

Papa Joe's Story

After our encounter with Round Man and his crew on Little Tybee, we knew we had a problem. We had to do something to save OUR island from those evil Atlanta developers. First, we did some research. Not very adventurous, but totally necessary. I hope I don't put you to sleep with this part of the story.

We went to the Tybee Library. The encyclopedia had information about environment and development. It included a write-up about a company named Kerr-McGee, a Texas mining company. Their claim to fame was putting the first oil drilling platforms in the Gulf of Mexico off the Louisiana coast just after World War II. The company had a lot of political clout because

36

its founder, Robert Kerr, was a United States Senator from Oklahoma and a close friend of President Lyndon Johnson. Now, remember that name, *Kerr-McGee*.

In the library I glanced up from my work and saw Mary Anderson shelving books on the other side of the room. She was one class behind me in school and was a volunteer at the library. I'd watched her from a distance many times. When she came over to ask if she could help, I couldn't get any words out. I had never spoken to her before. Willard told her what we were doing. She showed us how to use the card catalog and suggested some words we might use to find more information. That's how you had to look up books and information back then. No computers. No Google. There was an index for the newspaper, and you could find the stories on microfilm.

"Microfilm? Is that like film for one of those old cameras?" Jack interrupted.

"No. It's black and white pictures of a newspaper, magazine, or book by page on a reel of film. The reader you use enlarges the very small image so you can see it clearly. Back then it was a way to store lots on information in a small space."

I couldn't resist pointing to my phone, "Not as small as this."

We spent the afternoon reading about how important the marsh was to the health of the ocean. Some scientists from the University of Georgia living on Sapelo Island were doing research on the marsh, and one UGA professor wrote a textbook on ecology. The Tybee Library didn't have his textbook, and it probably would be beyond our seventh-grade science anyway. The research was helpful to understand the importance of the marsh, but for me, the time spent with Mary Anderson was even more important. You know, she was your grandmother, right?

I nodded with a big smile.

Well, back to the story. Willard knew more about government than the rest of us and suggested we attend a City Council meeting to see if anyone was talking about the future of OUR island. He even sat in on a deadly boring land-use committee meeting. Nothing. There was nothing on the agenda about Little Tybee Island.

Then Willard realized—Little Tybee wasn't in the Tybee city limits. The Chatham County Commission made the decisions affecting the island. None of us wanted to make the long bike ride into Savannah to talk to the county people. Instead, Willard knocked on the door of Ron White, the county commissioner who had a real estate office on Tybee. He had to wait a long time in the commissioner's outer office, before he got to ask some questions "for his 7th grade term paper" Papa Joe said, using air quotes.

Willard reported back to us, imitating the smooth real estate lawyer with his slicked, combed-back hair. "Yes, there is the possibility of development on the island. It's a little complicated for kids," Commissioner White drawled.

Willard did not rise to the insult but pressed for more details for his paper. "Who owned the land before and how did it get into the hands of Whitaker Construction?"

"They don't own it themselves but have partnered with Kerr-McGee, a mining company that thinks there's phosphate under the island and the marsh around it. After they get the phosphate out, they'll put the left-over material back in *pristine* condition for the construction of 20 new homes. The Kerr-McGee Company bought it from a wealthy Savannah developer, Jim Williams, three years ago, and they've been making their plans," Commissioner White said.

"When those plans are done, if they meet the building code, the Chatham County Commission will have no choice but to issue a permit, and the mining is likely to start before the end of this year," the commissioner said.

"The community will benefit from the mining jobs, and the construction of 20 homes will bring in some wealthy residents who can help us create more job opportunities," he proudly expounded with a self-satisfied and indulgent smile.

Willard thought about all the maids and workers who would be needed but asked a more important question. "How will people in the big homes get back and forth to the island?"

The commissioner sighed visibly. He really wanted this inquisitive 7th grader to go away. But he knew Willard's parents, aunts, and uncles were faithful voters. "At first they thought about a bridge, but neither the county nor the State of Georgia were gonna pay for it and the phosphate company didn't want to spend that kind of money. You know, eats away at profit," the commissioner explained with some patience.

"So, they've proposed a channel connecting through Jack's Cut to docks on the back side of Little Tybee. They have to dig out 100 to 150 feet of marsh mud to get to the phosphate, so they'll be close to having a channel when the mining is done anyway. Each home will have a dock. Residents will use golf carts to get around the island like they do on Hilton Head Island."

To Willard's dismay, the commissioner concluded, "There's not much we can do when people own the land. People have a right to do what they want with their land. There's no law on the books that'll stop 'em."

Commissioner White dismissed Willard with a warning, "You and your friends better stay away from the island. I'm sure Kerr-McGee won't like it if you trespass on their property. Good luck with that term paper, son. Say hey to your daddy for me."

"So, you knew the threat to the island was real," I interrupted.

"Yes, but we weren't gonna stay away from *our* island."

"So, what *did* you do?"

"That's a story for another day," Papa Joe said with a chuckle. "It's probably time to hit the sack. Let's get an early start tomorrow."

* * * * *

Jack

Chapter 8

The sun was already up when I opened my eyes, but it wasn't late. Out of my bedroom window I could see its rays had not yet hit the marsh. I could hear Papa Joe moving around downstairs.

I checked my phone. Only 7:15. There were messages from friends from last night.

"Cool video of you weaving that boat through the marsh. Looks like a deserted beach. No girls around?"

"You gone wild!"

"Sick!"

I responded, "It's nice to have a beach all to yourself, but it's the marsh that has me stoked. All kinds of animals living in the marsh grass. That giant dolphin was up close and personal."

I put the phone down and gazed out the window at the expansive marsh. I thought about what it would be like to hang with Papa Joe in the marsh and see more of it. But all of a sudden my nightmare came back to me.

There were little creatures swimming in the water and a large fish came along and swallowed them whole. Then around a curve in the marsh river came a huge mammal, not a cute dolphin, but one with a mouth full of sharp teeth. That mammal swallowed the fish and then headed right for the boat, swimming hard. Panicking, I couldn't get the engine started.

Luckily that dream had ended with a jerk. Awake, I remembered a few snippets from biology class. The

41

food chain pyramid where the big things ate the little things and where they were eaten by the biggest animal on the block. Somehow it all stayed in balance because the big things couldn't eat all the little things. If they did, there wouldn't be anything left for the next meal. Not as many big things would be able to live. But what about people? Where do they fit in? Scientists probably had a term for all that.

As I looked out on the marsh, grandpa's old boyhood campsite came to mind and incubated a plan for the day. Maybe we could do an overnight there.

When I came downstairs, Papa Joe was sitting at the kitchen table with his coffee cup in front of him. "What would you like to do today? Is it going to be water skiing?"

I shook my head, "No Papa Joe. Not today. Maybe another time." I plopped down on the chair opposite him.

"It was so amazing to see that dolphin yesterday! I was so excited last night I cracked open my computer and used your Wi-Fi to do some research."

"I do a little email on mine, but nothing I'd call research. I have to go to the library for that, Jack. Did you find anything interesting?"

"Did you know dolphins and a few other toothed whales are *echo locaters*?" I asked. "That means they send out energy waves or vibrations and get back an echo. From the echo they can tell how far away the object is and how big it is."

I was on a roll. "Bats are best known for this skill. Bats can actually send out 200 pulses per second and identify a two-millionth of a second difference in the echo. They use that to locate insects in the dark, and dolphins can identify fish beyond where they can see."

"Wow! I knew dolphins never ran into my Eco Tour boats, but I didn't know why. That also would be a great question on *Jeopardy*."

"*Jeopardy*?"

"Another time," Papa Joe said with a shake of his head. "How many pulses do the dolphins send out each second?"

"The article didn't give that. It was mainly on bats, but I'm sure I could find that out."

Papa Joe changed topics, "So what *is* the plan for today?"

"Well, I was wondering if you'd be up for this," I hesitated some. "Do you think we could camp out on Little Tybee like you and your friends did? Could we use the same spot?"

"Great!" He gave me two thumbs up and immediately went into planning mode. "Yes we can. I'm all in with that," he said. The idea came from me, but I suspected he had this idea in the back of his mind.

"We'll have to see what equipment in the back shed is still usable. I camped out a lot with your mother when she was young and a bit more with your grandmother, so I still have most of the equipment. I haven't used it much since then. Let's go look."

Things weren't in great shape, but we found an old Coleman stove, some fuel, a usable cooler, a little wire grill, and a box of pots and plates. The sleeping bags, sealed in plastic sheets to resist decay, looked good, and there were two small but usable tents.

"I think this is do-able," Papa Joe said. "Maybe a quick trip to the grocery store to stock up on a few things. Do you like peanut butter on a slice of bread? Nice and simple and meets the demand. I'll get some nice fresh veggies and a stick of butter to cook them in. I'll bring sausage and eggs. And potatoes. I love a big breakfast cooked over an open fire. I have a couple of blow-up mats in the upstairs closet that might make things a little more comfortable. How long should we plan to stay?"

"I'm thinking we try two nights; then see how it goes for a third?" I offered.

"Great." Papa Joe started ticking off what we'd need as if he had a checklist in his head. "We'll pack enough food for two days. We'll bring the rods and challenge ourselves to catch enough fish and other seafood to eat for a third. I'll fill the ice chest to keep our catch from spoiling and leave a little room for milk for cereal. Pick out a box of cereal you might like. We'll need some safety equipment: life preservers, a life-saving ring, and plenty of line. There's a story behind the line. I was once very glad we brought line and preservers when we camped there 50 years ago."

"What about a hammer or a crowbar?"

"Huh?"

"Maybe we can restore a little wildness? That shelf and its supports would look good in the campfire and aren't we supposed to be protecting the wild?" I suggested.

"I'm with you all the way," replied Papa Joe and gave me another thumbs up. "There's a hammer and a crowbar on the bench in the shed. Can't tidy it all up, but we might help DNR a little.

"We might need some extra gas if we're out there for three days. I'll put in an extra five-gallon can so we can explore some remote places in the marsh and maybe see another island. This small outboard engine takes you a long way on a little gas."

"I've also got some extra fuel for our phones," I contributed. "This little extra battery pack can charge my phone four times. Taking and sending videos uses lots of juice. Maybe it will be enough to keep our phones on for the three days."

"Good to know. That stuff's pretty new to me. You can get some good photos to send back to your mom and dad."

"And my friends. I don't know if any of them have ever camped on an island. Or camped anywhere. For most of them being away from home involves a hotel with a pool. I'd really like to get some cool videos to post on Instagram. Let them eat their hearts out."

"I'll bring my phone too. I'm sure my friends and your mother will want to keep up with us. No need for the old short-wave radio," Papa Joe chuckled. "Some good things have come along with all this change," he admitted. "I'm glad we can call for help if it's needed."

45

Chapter 9

I could see Papa Joe was not as nimble as the man who loomed large in my childhood memories. I remembered the captain of the *Mary Joe* as tall, tanned, lean, and as broad-shouldered as a commander of an Arctic expedition. His hair, naturally brown but bleached blond by days in the sun, now was no longer brown nor blond. It was replaced by white, creeping back on his forehead. He was still tanned, and his hair was long and wavy on the sides and in the back. He was a little stooped, and when he stepped down, I noticed he usually reached for a hand-hold.

"You do your exercises today, Papa Joe?" I asked as he came back into the kitchen, dressed and ready for adventure.

"Yes, just finished."

"What do you do?"

"I've modified some of the things our coach had us do in high school. Stretches, half-push-ups, squats, half sit-ups, and some curls with a small weight. How about you?"

"I'm not very athletic, but I'm impressed with what you do. Maybe I'll join you tomorrow and follow your routine."

We gathered our equipment and supplies into the boat. Papa Joe remembered to include some items because he once forgot them on his youthful adventures: a hatchet for firewood; matches; the cast net; a first aid kit; and binoculars.

I proudly told Papa Joe I had taken a first aid class in Boy Scouts and knew some basics. "I never had to use what I learned, but it makes me feel better that I know something basic."

"We're ready a little early today, and we won't get through the Cut for another hour, so let's try our luck with the rods on the way out. I got some frozen shrimp out of the freezer, and we could also try some of my old lures."

"You know," Papa Joe said with a serious tone, "we probably should call your mother and let her know what we're doing. Mothers aren't big on surprises. They're generally calmer when they know, or at least think they know. I called Willard a few minutes ago to let him know we're going to the old camp site. It's always good to let someone on shore know where to find you in the marsh."

Reluctantly, I agreed, "Calling Mom's a good idea, but I never know what to say to her. She's probably already at the office."

"Maybe you could ask how her real estate deal went. Asking questions is a good way to connect to people."

Mom answered on the second ring. For a fleeting moment her instincts went to worry. "Hi Hon. What's up? You good?"

"Yup. Papa Joe asked me to call and let you know our plans for the day. We're headed out to Little Tybee for a camping trip." I guess she could tell I was excited, and I gave her some of the details, which I'm sure she found even more unusual than the call. But I didn't tell her about operating the 15-horsepower outboard motor. No need to hear more cautioning. I really didn't want any advice from Mom.

"Sounds great, Jack. I loved those dad adventures when I was a kid. It's wonderful the marsh and the island are still the same. Take some good pictures. Put Papa Joe on for a minute." *Uh-oh*, I thought, but handed over the phone.

I could hear his side of the call. "Yes, yes, yes we have the life jackets and the ring; yes, I put the first-aid kit in; yes, there is now cell service from the island and the marsh; yes, we plan to be careful; yes, we'll call you if anything goes wrong." Unfortunately, family stories about his risk taking as a youth were true. He finally ended the call with "Love you. We'll stay in touch. Don't worry."

"Your mother was more adventuresome when she was your age. Probably the reason she's more cautious now."

"Hard to picture her as adventuresome," I commented.

As he was untying the boat, Papa Joe's phone started buzzing. He handed it to me. "Can you get that for me, please."

"Hello, this is Jack."

"Jack, this is Billy Wagner. Isn't your grandfather out of bed yet?"

"He's almost finished packing the boat for our camping trip. We're going to camp where you used to in the olden days. Shall I put him on?"

"No, young man. I can give you the news. I called my old boss at Coastal DNR about your injured dolphin, and they had me call NOAA Fisheries on their hot line. Wounded dolphins are their job. The National Oceanic Atmospheric Administration (NOAA) is responsible for enforcing the federal Marine Mammal Protection Act. Lots of discussion. Bottom line is, they know her, and maybe they'll mount a rescue effort."

"How do they know it's a girl and where she is?" I asked.

"From your photo they identified the markings

on her dorsal fin, and she popped out on their database. It's just like a fingerprint. They have satellite radios that track a dolphin's location if the dolphin has a tracker. This one doesn't, but she's part of a small marsh pod frequenting the creeks off the Tybee Slough. She's been in trouble before, so they know a lot about her. The last time they had eyes on her they thought she might be pregnant."

Billy explained their concern for the dolphin now. "The fishing line may cut deeply into her fin and be life threatening. The fin gives her stability in the water. She can operate without it, but if the fishing line severs an artery in the front of the fin, it could kill her. She's just like a human in that respect. They're getting a veterinarian to review your photo and will quickly make a decision about what to do."

"Wow! That's amazing." I had more questions, "When will they know if a rescue's needed? Did they have any advice for us?"

"While you're in the area, keep an eye out for her. They may send someone out to observe her, but if you get a sighting, take some more pictures. Another video would help them evaluate," Billy suggested.

"NOAA's Southeastern office is bringing a large group of experts together on a zoom call to review the case. They'll make some decisions tomorrow. I gave Joe's number to the Stranding Coordinator, and you may hear directly from her. It would be tragic to lose this dolphin in our local marsh. She's young but already has a big family and can have more babies in the future. I'll let you know if I hear more."

"You know I'd love to be part of that."

"I'm sure you would. I'll let you know if, when, and where. In the meantime, you take good care of that old man. He's a precious soul. Give me your number so I have two phones to try." I saved Billy's number in my contacts. *Never know when you might need some help from civilization.*

Wouldn't it be great if we could help in the rescue? I bet that would be the top story of spring break, I thought as we pulled away from the dock.

Adventure! I could see Papa Joe felt he was young again, remembering his days of living free on the edge of the ocean. Billy's comment gave me a glimmer of some future responsibilities that might be just around a looping marsh creek. Maybe I'd already helped identify a wounded dolphin. Maybe I'd have to save some other marsh critter or even a human critter. With lots of gas and two days of food, adventure lay ahead.

Chapter 10

Before we entered the Cut, with the sun at our back, we tried for trout and sea bass along the far side of the Back River. A few pelicans were dive-bombing near the marsh edge. If these birds were there, Papa Joe said it was likely a good place to fish.

"Hey, I think I've got something," I exclaimed as I felt a bite. Unfortunately, my tug wasn't quick enough to get the fish hooked. "Oops, there he goes." That moment was repeated several times. I was not a patient fisherman. Yet.

"I generally have better luck when I fish where the tide is flowing out. I learned that from watching the dolphins. Maybe later we should try the back side of Little Tybee when the tide is moving out," Papa Joe offered.

The tide waters were climbing up the marsh grass, so now there was plenty of clearance for a boat, even a loaded boat, in the Cut. We picked up some more oyster clumps on our way towards our campsite.

"Let's see if we can find that dolphin again," I suggested. Papa Joe let me steer the boat as we meandered, exploring a few marsh streams. But no sign of the dolphin.

By early afternoon we arrived at the campsite. It was a warm, sunny day with a nice breeze coming onshore out of the northeast, pushing any early spring insects back into the marsh and away from our site. The flat spot under the sprawling live oak was perfect for the tents. Other campers had left a nice ring of rocks for the campfire. According to Papa Joe, storms usually came out of the northeast, so the back side of the island was the place to be if the wind and the heavy rain came in from the sea. The dunes along the beach side of the island protected the camp, but you had to keep a close eye to the northeast because most coastal storms didn't give much warning.

We ate the ham-and-cheese sandwiches we'd brought and then went around the end of the island to see if the tide had deposited anything new on the beach. I was hoping for something interesting left by others, maybe a sailor's cap, a bottle with a note, some sign of a shipwreck. We only found a pair of half-buried sunglasses and one moldy flip-flop. In my mind I created the people who belonged to them. I could see them running away from a threatening island hermit.

Reality was much tamer. We did find more empty whelk shells and three unbroken sun-bleached sand dollars. A hollowed-out Horseshoe Crab shell. The big find was a huge clam shell. Papa Joe pointed out that by imagining the flow of water through the shell you could see how a bivalve functions.

A starfish lay at the edge of the water. I picked it up and threw it beyond the breaking waves. That brought a nod of approval. "It's a good thing to do even though there are many more that get washed up. It's like the old lady said when she peed in the ocean, 'Every little bit counts.'"

I laughed. Papa Joe wasn't a big joke teller, and when an unexpected one came out, it was especially funny. I could tell that was an old standby he used with his friends.

"Let's go back and try the rods near camp. It would be wonderful to have some fresh fish for tonight's dinner. The tide's starting to flow out, and I think there'll be whiting and trout patrolling the stream bed where the marsh empties out."

With our old marsh shoes on, we waded out from the edge of the sand bar, and using a few shrimp pieces, cast our lines into the flow. It turned out to be a great spot. Within a few minutes we had three whiting and two trout.

"Papa Joe, take my phone and get one of those few-second videos of me casting my line right here. My friends need to see this. Like before, touch the large red button to start and the small red button to stop."

"And your mom?"

"OK" I responded reluctantly.

I looked at the footage. "You got it! The shakiness will give a realistic feel on Instagram. I think I'll call this *Jack in the Wilderness Installment #2*. You get more likes or views when you give your post a title. This way they can follow my adventures day by day."

"Does that include your mother?"

"Probably not. She's not much on social media. For her, computers are just for legal documents and legal research."

Looking at the catch, I quickly changed the subject. "We're gonna feast tonight!!"

"That we will. Let's stop now. Remember, we don't take more out of nature than we can use. Let's clean and fillet these and put them in the cooler for later."

"Clean? Fillet them?"

"Yes. You can't eat the guts, the bones, or the scales."

I easily picked up on this new skill of cleaning fish to add to my coastal repertoire. I was curious about scales.

"Some fish have a protective coat that is like little clear shingles." Papa Joe explained. "You can't eat the ridged plates."

With the cleaned fish in the small ice chest, Papa Joe suggested, "Let's do some more exploring." We started the motor and steered through the channel to the open ocean. It was a calm day with just two- and three-foot swells the boat could easily handle.

Papa Joe got into his tour-guide mode and started explaining things to me. "Sand along the coast is always moving south and creating new sandbars. Eventually the sand buildup stays above the high tide. Then the tide adds dead cordgrass to the sand, and that's the beginning of soil and then small plants. It's a fascinating process and gives the shoreline a changing look. Sometimes, over the years you get a new island."

The lecture mode didn't bother me much. I knew he used to make his living as a coastal tour guide, and it felt good to let him go back to that life for a moment. When we hit the open water of the Wassaw Sound, we turned back north as the sun was moving lower.

"That's Wassaw Island in the distance," Papa Joe pointed out. "A man named George Parsons bought that island on his honeymoon as a gift for his bride. The Parsons family decided they wanted to protect it from development, so they put it under an environmental easement, sold it to the Nature Conservancy, who sold it to the state of Georgia. The family kept a little compound in the middle for their own use, but the rest of the island is open to the public—if you can get there by boat."

"Environmental easement? What's that?" I asked.

"It's a legal agreement the owner makes not to change the island. It can stay that way for a thousand years no matter who owns it. Ask you mother about it or look it up on your iPad."

Actually, I was more interested in exploring the

island. "Could we go out there?"

"I'm afraid we're running out of time, and I don't want to get too far out in open water in this small boat. Maybe another boat, another day. But you know, if somebody hadn't decided to protect that island, we'd be driving there on a causeway like your friends did to get to Hilton Head. It would be just like another Hilton Head."

"Is that part of your story?" I asked.

"Not exactly. It did happen about the same time as the big fight with Kerr-McGee over mining Little Tybee and a lot of Wassaw Sound where we are now. Most of the islands along Georgia's coast were owned by wealthy families, and each has a different story about keeping them protected. That would make an interesting book."

Back at the campsite, we cooked the fish slowly on the charcoal grill while two potatoes wrapped in foil lay among the coals. We added a few sticks of wood from the dismantled shelf, and the fire blazed up as we savored the tender fish fillets.

I polished off my last bite, stretched out on the sand with my hands behind my head. "That was wonderful. Kudos to the master chef.

"So, tell me more of how you and your friends saved Little Tybee," I suggested.

* * * * * *

Papa Joe's Story

A dramatic adventure that's part of the story started right here at this campsite, Papa Joe picked up where he had left off.

One late afternoon when we were sure Round Man and his crew were gone, we went back out to the campsite to spend the night. We intended to pull up all those survey stakes. Then the Whitaker crew and Round Man would've had to come back out and do it all over again. That might create a fuss and get people's attention about what that company was planning for *our* island.

There was a problem that day. We weren't payin' attention to the weather. After setting up camp in the fading light, we saw the dark clouds building up from the northeast. The wind was picking up. That meant we were **not** going back home that night. We had learned enough to prepare for sudden summer squalls. Always carried extra gear. Now we double-staked our tent, put another set of mooring lines on the boat, and threw a few sticks of wood into the back of the tent to keep them dry. Then we radioed the Coast Guard Station to let them know where we were and to alert our parents that we were safe. The station operator said to "Stay put. Don't try to come home. Storm's big on our radar."

We were ready when it hit. Eight- to ten-foot swells, and the storm had come at near high tide. The waves crashed hard along the beach side of the island. In our tent, protected by the dunes and a hundred feet of maritime forest, we felt secure, but wary. The island took a pounding at the high point in the storm. Nobody slept.

The radio crackled.

"Coast Guard here. Come in, campers. Over."

"Roger that," we replied.

"Y'all safe?"

"Roger, buttoned up and tied down. Over."

"Be aware there may be a sailboat in trouble off the southern tip of your island. This storm and the sand bars will keep our rescue boat out of the area for a while. Seas too high for small boats and can't risk hitting those hidden sandbars. Please advise if you see something. Be safe. Over."

"Roger, Coast Guard. Will advise. Over"

Willard turned to us and said, "Let's get our rain gear and check out the other side."

When we got there, through the horizontal sheets of rain we could barely make out a 30- to 35-foot sailboat over on its side. The waves were battering its full length. Stuck on a sand bar, it wasn't going anywhere anytime soon.

"Do you see any people in the water?" Billy yelled.

"Yes. I see two men hanging onto the mast on the lee side of the boat." I yelled back.

Willard, the athlete, took charge. "Get all the extra line from our boat and bring it here with the life saver ring. I'm going out there, and we're going to bring those two guys in."

From the beach, Billy and I served as anchors for the line tied firmly around Willard. Carrying another line attached to a lifesaving ring, he walked into the surf holding the ring over his head. A big wave knocked him over, and he disappeared under the surging surf. With all our might we pulled him toward the beach. He came back up when his feet caught the edge of a sandbar. Now he could stand up enough to swing the lifesaving ring around his body.

Willard threw it with all his might and almost toppled over again. The older man lunged for it. Missed! Willard pulled it in and threw it again. The man lunged again, and this time grabbed on. We pulled Willard. And Willard pulled the man. They struggled through the breaking waves, and with a lot of groans we pulled them both to the top of the foaming, but stable sand.

Willard went right back out. The next man was younger and quicker and swam a little way out to catch the ring. Again, we hauled at that line until the man's feet hit the sand and he stumbled to the top of the beach, gasping for breath.

We were all exhausted but knew it was important to get to shelter. Moving quickly to our campsite on the protected side of the island, we stripped off the wet clothes and wrapped ourselves and our "guests" in sleeping bags and blankets. When the rain subsided, we got a fire blazing with the dry wood from inside our tent.

The radio squawked, "Please report."

"All safe," replied Willard. "We pulled two sailors from the sea. All warm by the fire with extra blankets now. Sailboat still on its side, stuck on a sandbar. Please advise. Over."

"If no immediate risk, stay put till morning. We'll send a boat just after daybreak. Great work, guys."

As Billy and I warmed ourselves and dozed off now and then, Willard stayed up, kept the fire going, and as usual, started asking questions.

"Who are you guys? What happened?"

"I'm James McHenry, and this here's Randall Bennett. I've been around this coast all my life. My family's been here for generations. I own and publish the *Savannah Morning Post*. For years we've been running stories of mishaps off the coast. You'd think I'd know better," he said, shaking his head at his own mistake.

"We came out of the Intracoastal Waterway and into the ocean through Wassaw Sound for a long afternoon sail north. Beautiful day. No storms predicted. We had even checked with the Coast Guard. That storm was sudden! When it hit us, we couldn't get the sails down. From a half mile off the end of Tybee, the wind drove us southeast into those sand bars. Those suckers keep shifting, you know. They're like the end of a fishhook, catching everything coming at them."

Mr. McHenry ruefully shook his head, "Should've

struck the sails quicker. Hey, if it weren't for you guys, we'd still be trying to stay with the sailboat. Don't know how long I could've held on. The water's still mighty cold. Thanks again for your quick thinking and strong backs. You must know a lot about this area."

Billy piped up, "All three of us have grown up on Tybee and seen the Atlantic in all its moods. We love this place, and our parents schooled us from when we were little runts. They trust us out here."

"From my perspective your folks are right to trust you," Mr. McHenry said. "I might not be here without you." We all noticed he did not say "boys."

Always putting things together, Willard spoke up in a rush of words. "We have a special mission, and maybe you could help. We discovered some company from Atlanta may be up to no good out here. They're surveyin' this island, puttin' stakes in the sand like they're markin' off house lots."

Awake now, I jumped into the story. "They're also drilling to see what's under the island, and the new owner is Kerr-McGee, a mining company from Texas. We don't want that to happen. Our short-term plan was to make the stakes go away," I admitted. "But we know more people need to know what's going to happen here."

"The storm may have helped us there," Willard continued. "But we mean to save Little Tybee so we can keep on camping and fishing here. This is *our* island and not some mining site. We'd like Whitaker and Kerr-McGee, whoever they are, to go away."

Mr. McHenry turned to his companion, a political reporter with the paper, and asked, "Randall, you know anything about this?"

"I had a couple of conversations with some coastal scientists on Sapelo," Randall Bennett replied. But we haven't been able to get any further confirmation."

"Well, we talked to Chatham County Commissioner White, and he confirmed what we saw with our own eyes. I put it in my 7th grade term paper," Willard offered.

"OK. If we can get confirmation of this story, I can assure you my reporters will follow it up to the end. There's no way we should be mining this beautiful coast. Randall, you're on this story until this project is dead!"

The Coast Guard arrived the next morning with a photographer on board, and we were on the front page of the *Savannah Morning Post*. Luckily the part about our survey-stake removal plan did not make the news story. Kerr-McGee didn't make the story either, but we knew when the paper got the scoop on the full story, it would be on the front page.

"So, that's how you saved this island?" I asked.

"No, no. Getting the attention of the newsmen was a good start, but it took a lot more than that to save the island," Papa Joe concluded.

What else could there be? I wondered.

* * * * * *

Chapter 11

Papa Joe lapsed into silence. We lay on the sand facing the Atlantic's endless horizon, looking up at the stars.

"Wow! Look at all the stars. We don't have all this in Atlanta."

"Actually, you do," Papa Joe chuckled. "The stars are always there. You just can't see them for all the bright lights of the big city. Look around, there's very little light from the earth here except across the way on Tybee and way off behind us in Savannah."

"There it is," I pointed. "I can always find the Big Dipper and the North Star. Maybe that cluster over there to the right is the Little Dipper."

Papa Joe pointed to three stars close together. "I think that's Orion's belt."

"Orion, huh? He was some Greek god or something, wasn't he? It's funny, it almost seems like this place and Atlanta are not on the same map. Maybe not the same planet."

"Seeing all this makes you remember how big the universe is," Papa Joe mused. "My old friend, Willard, the scientist, loves to get talking about all the physics theories explaining the nature of our universe. I don't understand him most of the time. Have you studied any of those theories?"

"Not much. I kind of tuned out when our science teacher was explaining quantum theory and wave theory. And there's this new thing called string theory. I guess that's some way to tie the other theories together."

"Nice pun, Jack."

"My science teacher was very excited about this new telescope the space agency has sent up to operate beyond our atmosphere. The Webb Space Telescope is larger than the old one, and its lookout site is one million miles from earth. It may be able to see light from the edge of the universe. She said it will see light that started out a million years ago."

"I told Willard that, and he corrected me. They think it'll see light from the beginning of the universe—they think that was 13.7 *billion* years ago. Maybe they'll see something in black holes or watch a star when it dies. I understand why scientists are excited to find out things we don't know."

"That could be pretty cool, but I don't know if I'm smart enough to be one of those scientists."

"Well," Papa Joe said, clearing his throat a little, "I think people should just go one step at a time. Follow what interests you. Don't worry about the challenges that might be ahead of you."

The conversation was beginning to sound like advice to me. I changed the subject. "So, this is the spot where you rescued Mr. McHenry and his reporter."

"Yes. It wasn't so quiet then, and there wasn't any space to lie back on the beach. See where the waves are breaking now? There are still sand bars there, a little higher today. They come out of the water at low tide to form little temporary resting islands for birds flying north."

"Still dangerous?" asked Jack.

"On both sides of high tide you can't see them. You have to go out half a mile to get enough water under your keel to get into the channel carved by the Back River to turn toward Tybee Island. Wind from the northeast directly off the end of Tybee can produce some powerful waves just a couple yards to seaward."

For a while we both just gazed at the overwhelming heavens wrapped in stars—so peaceful and quiet. Papa Joe broke the silence, "It's hard for me to imagine your life in Atlanta. I've lived almost my whole life on Tybee. Every time I've been to Atlanta everything seems to be rush, rush, rush—lots of people and traffic. What's it like for you, Jack?"

"Like Mom told you, we live in a nice neighborhood, and I have friends there. We go to school together. We ride bikes a lot in the neighborhood, but if we want to go to a concert somewhere, one of our parents has to drive. There are lots of things to do so I can't wait to be old enough to drive myself. I know Mom is *not* looking forward to that day."

"Is there quiet?"

"Not like this," I said a little wistfully. "There are lots of sirens in the night, but you get so you don't hear them. Traffic noise comes from a nearby interstate, and the state highway a block away. People commuting to work cut through the neighborhood driving too fast, ignoring the stop sign on our corner. There's always lots of construction too."

Papa Joe decided to push the conversation a bit more. I got the sense he wanted to know more about me, this grandson from the city. "So, until you can get a driver's license, how do you spend your time? What kind of things do you like to do?"

"Well, I like my video games. I play against my friends normally. During the pandemic I spent a lot more time with a few friends zooming and face-timing. I was online a lot. My classes were all online. But that was OK. I liked the chance to keep ahead of my assignments and work on things at my own pace. I know that wasn't true for many of my friends, but it worked OK for me."

I interrupted myself, "Hey, thanks for contributing to my little fund that let me buy the parts and build my own computer."

"Glad to help."

"I do worry about some of the kids at my school," I said quietly. "During the pandemic if you didn't live in a family with lots of computers and a quiet place to work, you didn't do well with online school. Lots of kids need more. A face on a screen did not cut it, so some kids got behind."

"I'm glad you see that, Jack."

I shifted subjects, "I'm learning to play a trumpet, and I'm in the junior-high orchestra. That didn't work so well during the pandemic, looking at a computer screen. Couldn't have a zoom orchestra practice. But now that we're back in school, I look forward to the practice sessions, and we'll have a performance soon."

"Do you think you'll like it enough to play in the band when you get to high school?"

"Maybe. It takes a lotta practice, and I don't want to miss out on other cool things. Last year my dad took me to a University of Georgia football game, and I loved watching the Red Coat Marching Band perform at half time. Now *that* would be very cool—to be part of that band someday. I liked it better than the game."

Papa Joe asked another question, "So what about your dad? How do you two get along?"

"He's OK. Busy, like Mom. I can't remember us ever laying down in the back yard and looking at the stars. I *am* proud of him though."

After a few seconds I continued. "You know he's an engineer. He heads a Georgia Power team that moves into communities damaged by severe storms, and they get the power back on. Last year he was on the Mississippi Gulf coast for a month and a half. It was hard. Mom and I had to work together more. He did call often, but that's not the same as being home."

"A family certainly has to pull together," Papa Joe responded. "Lots of things can pull families apart, and being in separate places is one of those. The war pulled me away from here and from Mary."

"I never heard you talk about the war," I said, a bit surprised that he brought it up.

"My generation's war was in Vietnam. When I graduated from high school, I was hoping to marry your grandmother, but the Selective Service Board said I had to go to Vietnam first. Thinking of her kept me alive while I was over there." He added quietly, "That didn't work for a good number of my friends from back here or several of my army buddies."

"What's the Selective Service?"

"It's better known as the draft," Papa Joe explained. "Under the rules, when you turn a certain age, it used to be 18, you signed up with the Selective Service. That meant the local draft board could select you and require you to go off to war. It wasn't a very fair system, but I went when they selected me."

"Tell me more about the war, the fighting."

"I'd rather not ..." Papa Joe went quiet. "I can't, Jack. I try not to dredge up those memories. They hurt too much. It's not you. Maybe someday when you're a little older. Oh, I hate playing that 'older' thing on you. The 'older' excuse reminds me of Round Man calling us 'boys.' I want you to know I don't see you that way. It's just me. I don't want to talk about it to anybody. Things happen in a war that are very hard to talk about."

I could see the talk of war was a little tough on Papa Joe and decided to switch subjects. We were both getting good at switching subjects when there was a need. "So, what else happens on this beach at night?"

"Your grandmother and I came across the Back River in our runabout and walked out here in the moonlight a few times. Our first kiss happened here," Papa Joe said. I could feel him smiling in the dark. "But mainly the quiet happens. Occasionally, if you have a good flashlight, you can see a ghost crab looking for food at all hours of the night. The big event is a visit from female Loggerhead Turtles. They come out of the ocean and flipper their way up the beach to a spot above the high tide line, scrape the sand back, lay their eggs, bury them, and flipper their way back to the water."

"Can we find some tomorrow?"

"Not tomorrow. It's too early in the year. They don't start depositing eggs until warmer weather. Not till May. Even then it takes watching all night, and you still might not see one dragging herself across the sand. In the morning you can tell where the nest is by following the tracks."

I had more questions. "When do the babies come out of the eggs?"

"It takes 55 to 60 days if all goes well. There are raccoons here, and they're always on the hunt for a nest. Some nests have up to 120 eggs."

"Wow! That's a lot of eggs and baby turtles. With so many babies what is the problem? Shouldn't there be lots of turtles swimming in the ocean?" I asked.

"They need a lot of eggs because most hatchlings don't make it to adulthood. Some environmental groups, trying to preserve the loggerheads, send dedicated young people out here to mark the nests and protect them—at least from people. They put a net over the nest to keep some predators from digging up the eggs. The turtle protectors are not big raccoon fans, and they don't like people who bring their dogs here to run wild. When the little ones hatch, they head toward the ocean."

Puzzled, I asked, "How do they know which way to go? Do they have some kind of built-in GPS?"

"You could call it that. At night the ocean is lighter than the dune-lined shoreline," Papa Joe explained. "They're running toward the light like their ancestors. But we humans are messing with their GPS. The light from human development along the shore can confuse the baby turtles' compass and get them moving in the wrong direction. If they get moving in the wrong direction, they often end up as road kill."

"So out here on this undeveloped island they're likely to get going in the right direction," I concluded.

"Yes, but there are still a lot of casualties along the way. They have to evade the gauntlet of beach predators: the ghost crabs, raccoons, larger sandpipers and other sea birds. It takes a lot of nests to keep the turtle population stable. One summer I counted 50 nests on this island alone. Scientists are always trying to figure out what we humans could and should do to help."

"Speaking of doing—What are we doing tomorrow?" I asked, ready to move on from the turtle discussion.

"We'll begin with camping duties—more wood gathering and keeping the place neat. Then, like most animals in the wild, we'll start thinking about food first. It'll probably be time to pull the crab traps out of the stream and see if we had a good spot, and I want some more fish to cook on the fire tomorrow night."

"Maybe we could explore a couple of those hummocks?" I suggested.

"That's a good idea. I'd like you to see the little periwinkles doing their farming on the cordgrass stems. Maybe we'll see a Great Blue Heron, an Egret, or find the nest of the Bald Eagle we met the other day. I think her nest is high in a pine tree a little way up our creek from here. The eagles seem to be making a comeback around here. Back in the 80s when Billy worked for the DNR, they didn't find any nests, and this year the DNR count found 73 nests on the coast."

"It's OK with me if we just go exploring," I said. "Maybe keep an ear cocked for those Clapper Rails."

We went back to the campsite and policed the fire—putting on one large piece of wood to smolder through the night so it would light easily in the morning. The smoke would also help keep down the pesky insects, and the small breeze coming from the ocean would help.

We sat by the fire while the new wood flamed up. I wasn't ready for the day to come to an end.

"Papa Joe, tell me what happened when your picture was in the newspaper? Did your teacher see it? Did you become famous on the island?" I asked.

* * * * *

Papa Joe's Story

Yes. We got a little attention. Everybody who lived on the island knew who we were. Now this part of the story really might put you to sleep.

Mrs. Peabody, our seventh-grade teacher, saw our picture in the paper. On Monday morning she made us stand up in front of the class and tell the full story. Billy did most of the talking about the rescue, but when it came to what we'd learned about the threat to Little Tybee and the marsh, Willard took over. He told everybody what Round Man and his drilling team said and what Commissioner White had to say. There was a little booing in the back of the room when Willard came to the Commissioner. I didn't say much but asked the class to tell their parents about Kerr-McGee and think about what we could do to stop their mining operation.

Mrs. Peabody liked the discussion. While the environment of the marsh was not in her lesson plans, I think she found this to be one of those "teachable moments." She asked the whole class to join the research efforts and find out something new about the marsh, the island, and any laws that might help save the island. And of course, "write a paper" on what they found. With her it was always "write a paper." We got a few dirty looks from classmates.

I thought it was great. Now the whole class was working on this, and maybe they'd get their parents involved. Anyway, Billy, Willard and I were in this fight, and it was nice to have the class with us. We didn't plan to lose.

Boy, did Mrs. Peabody get enthusiastic. She had lived on Tybee most of her life and was very interested in the environment. She knew one of the University of Georgia scientists who did research on the marsh and lived on Sapelo Island. She said she'd invite him to speak to the class.

Willard picked up on that idea, "Hey, if the scientist is coming, we should invite other people on the island to hear what he has to say. We could even do it at night." Mrs. Peabody would check with Principal Thomas about an evening presentation, but thought maybe the PTA could help to get some of the parents to come.

Every day we looked in the *Savannah Morning Post* for stories by our friendly reporter, Mr. Bennett. Our newfound interest in the news certainly surprised our parents. I suggested going to the island at night and trying to disable some of Round Man's equipment, maybe put a little sugar in the gasoline tank of the drilling machine. But Willard, who was often the wiser voice among us, said that would not solve the problem and might disable us instead. "Better to keep the focus on the issue rather than our arrest," he said.

The newsman came through. On Friday morning the *Post* had a front-page story, with a map and everything. You couldn't miss it. Every reader got a full picture of what was going on. Most people back then read the newspaper.

Kerr-McGee and their fancy Atlanta lawyers had been to see Governor Lester Maddox and asked to lease 72,000 acres around our island. They owned Little Tybee, but that was not enough to make a big profit on the phosphate. They even wanted control of three miles off the beach. They were going to dig out the phosphate, which was 100 feet below the island, and they'd pile that marsh mud (they called it "overburden") and make dry land to build new seaside homes. Probably that's why our real estate agent/county commissioner was supporting the project. The governor had invited newspaper reporters from Atlanta and Savannah into his office, and they heard the whole presentation.

At first during the meeting, Governor Maddox was very excited about the jobs the mining operation would produce in Savannah, but some of the officials who knew the importance of the marsh asked him to slow down. In the end he asked the Attorney General, Arthur Bolton, to hold two public hearings: one in Atlanta and one in Savannah. Maddox said he wanted to know what the people thought about the proposal. The Governor also wanted to know what the scientists thought the mining would do to the coast, and so he asked the head of the University System to study the impact of the proposal. That was way before federal officials cared much about our environment.

When we got to class the next Monday, Mrs. Peabody was very excited. She held up a copy of the *Post* and read the whole story to the class. She wanted all the students to have the same information. Not everybody's family could afford a newspaper.

Billy was all excited too. He planned to go to the hearing in Savannah—it was for everybody, and maybe we could let them know this island was important to us. The governor had probably never been to Little Tybee. Maybe he would come and see for himself.

The hearing in Savannah was a month off. "If you go to a hearing, you ought to know what you're talking about," Mrs. Peabody said. "Your papers are due in a week, and you need to take a position on this proposal. The company says they are going to create jobs, and y'all know there are not many good jobs around here. If they do it right, they say there could be a very pretty beach just across the Back River."

We knew Mrs. Peabody was just trying to get all of us to think a little deeper and do more research. She also knew a pretty beach would be attractive because often the industrial and city sewer waste coming out of the Savannah River smelled up our Tybee beach. Sometimes it was even closed to swimming.

With some fanfare, she also announced her scientist friend from Sapelo Island was coming to talk to people in Savannah next week and could make a presentation on Tybee Wednesday evening in the school's assembly hall.

Willard was over the moon with excitement at that news. He'd loved every science class since we were in first grade. Our little campaign would get some new facts we could publicize.

"We gotta get all our parents and other grown-ups on the island to come hear this scientist. We could write a one-page flyer and send it home with the school kids this afternoon," Billy declared.

Mrs. Peabody slowed him down just a little. "Billy, you work on that tonight and bring it in tomorrow morning and show it to the rest of the class. I'll check with the principal this afternoon about sending it home tomorrow. Now, take out your math books and turn to the chapter on percentages." There was a little grumbling in the back of the class.

Billy's flyer went home with the students the next day.

About 125 people showed up to hear Dr. Lane Alexander. A tall slender man with bushy hair, he was a lot younger than we all expected. Mrs. Peabody had asked Commissioner White to do the introductions. I thought that was a smart way to make sure the commissioner heard what the scientist had to say and see the number of people on the island who were not happy with the Kerr-McGee mining proposal.

Dr. Alexander worked with a team of scientists at the University of Georgia Marine Institute on Sapelo Island. They actually lived on the island. They'd been studying the marshland and ocean life around the island for more than 15 years and shared research with scientists all over the world.

For Willard, sitting in the front row, this was the coolest thing that could happen. Dr. Alexander talked for a while and then spent lots of time answering questions. And there were a LOT of questions. His big point was that the marshland along the Georgia coast was the source of most of the life in the ocean. The tiny animals growing in the marsh were the food supply for all the bigger fish and mammals that lived in the deeper ocean waters. Without the marsh, there would be no shrimp, no sea trout, no sharks— a little cheer from some of the kids—no dolphins and no whales. We weren't sure back then what he meant by "ecology," but it was clear a lot of things in the ocean would die if the marsh and its tiny inhabitants were not producing plenty of food.

Kerr-McGee said they were going to build a pipeline three miles out from the beach to take the bad left-over parts of the phosphate process out to sea and away from the beach. "We know, that won't work," Dr. Alexander said. "One of our team of scientists studies currents, and he said the currents along the Georgia coast would push the bad stuff right back onto the beaches."

Kerr-McGee also said they would put the marsh back in pristine condition when the phosphate was out. "Mother Nature took thousands of years to create the rich marsh mud, and it's unlikely scientists could use the dried up mud from the mining to create new marshes," Dr. Alexander pointed out.

"Don't mess with Mother Nature," a kid in the audience called out. Everyone laughed—even the commissioner.

Well, everyone left the meeting convinced the mining proposal was a bad idea. I saw Commissioner White go out the side door of the auditorium. He didn't stay around for his usual hand-shaking.

Willard was worried the hearing in Savannah might be on a school day, but I said it could be part of our research for Mrs. Peabody. She would probably get us an excuse or assign us a report. And she did. She was a very cool teacher who seemed to love it when her students were learning something new, even if it was not in the classroom or in the textbook.

I went up to Dr. Alexander after the meeting and asked him what we could do to stop the mining. He said, "From the looks of this meeting, you boys have done a lot already. Only a few people make the decisions, but they also listen closely to what regular people have to say. I hope you come to the hearing and get your feelings in front of the committee. I'm with you all the way. All the other Sapelo scientists are also committed, and we'll be at the hearing. You let me know if I can help you in any way."

"Can we call you if we have other questions," Willard asked.

"Yes, please do. Here's my card with my phone number on the island. You have to get to our island by boat, but we do have phones. If I'm doing field work, I'll call you back when I get in."

As he was leaving the cafeteria, Dr. Alexander turned and added one more suggestion. "You know, Governor Maddox often says he wants to hear what the little people have to say. In fact, he has a Little People's Day at the Capitol and says he'll listen to anyone who shows up. Why don't you and your friends go see him?"

Well, that was like waving a red flag in front of a bull for Billy. Why wait in line at the hearing when they could go right to the top man himself.

* * * * * *

Knowing there was more story to come, we both relaxed in the silence, pleased with the day. Darkness settled around us so I tucked away my sketch pad, which had been a comfortable distraction while listening to stories. The fire had burned down enough to leave it on its own in the stone ring. As I crawled into my sleeping bag, I was thinking of eagles, crabs, storm rescues, and the great adventures just around a bend in the marsh. *What was Papa Joe was thinking about?*

Chapter 12

When I crawled out of the tent the next morning, Papa Joe already had the fire blazing and was frying some bacon and scrambling eggs. With his coffee cup in his hand, he signaled for me to get a plate. "I think this is going to be a big day, and we should start with a big, tasty camping-out breakfast. I love cooking outdoors."

"I'm ready for it all," I said enthusiastically just as Papa Joe's phone buzzed.

"I got it." I said.

" Hello, this is Jack."

"Jack, this is Jane Olmstead from the National Oceanographic and Atmospheric Agency. Everybody calls us NOAA for short. Are you the dolphin photographer?"

"Yes ma'am, that's me. Are you connected to the Noah who built the Ark?"

Jane laughed, "I may have heard that one before. No, very different time and different Noah. But we've one thing in common. We like to save animals who are threatened.

"So, getting to the purpose of my call, I heard from Billy Wagner that you and your grandfather were going to be camping out in the Little Tybee marsh. Are you there now?"

"Yes ma'am. We're at the south end of Little Tybee on the back side behind some dunes. Our boat's tied up just off the Tybee Slough. We're planning to be here for a couple more days."

"Good. I want you to be on the lookout for Z-28 today. We know who the dolphin is and that she usually stays in the creeks off the Slough and with the high tide she'll hunt north toward the Tybee Causeway. We need some closer observations, but I don't have anyone who can get there today. Your pictures are great, and a few more from different angles could help us make a decision about how quickly we should move."

"My Papa Joe has been in and out of the marsh most of his life, and I'm sure we can track her down."

"I'm sure he knows not to get too close. Dolphins are very friendly to us humans, but we can disturb them if we get too pushy. We don't want her to run from us if we have to do a rescue. This is my cell phone, so put it in your contacts and use it to send any new pictures you may get. I hope you're enjoying your adventure with your granddad, and we don't interfere with your time together."

"We're both looking for adventure, and working to help a dolphin fits. I'll let you know if we have a sighting today."

"Thanks, Jack. Great talking to you. Keep up the good work."

Papa Joe finished cooking, and we sat down with our plates on a convenient log. I told my grandfather about the call from Jane Olmstead. "Wouldn't it be great if we could help in the rescue? I bet that'd be my school's top story of spring break!"

In the meantime, we needed to fish for our supper. The fishing in the Slough near the campsite continued to be great. After a half hour with my rod and the shrimp, I had enough for dinner—three trout and one whiting. I cleaned them and put them on ice while Papa Joe cleaned up from the meal.

"You're getting good at this. You may be a fisherman for life. Let's get the boat going and go pull the crab traps."

We cleaned the camp, made some sandwiches, checked the boat fuel supply, and made ready to leave. "Jack, take the stern seat and operate the outboard today."

Papa Joe gave me some instructions. "Just remember the experience from the other day. Make small steady changes to the rudder and the throttle. You can get in trouble when you make big quick changes. Slow and steady is the way to go. Make sure it's in neutral and clear of the bottom when you give the starter rope a firm pull. You know it'll take a couple of tries."

It took great effort to pull fast enough for the engine to start. It finally started on the third pull. I put it in reverse and backed slowly out of the little creek. We went north up the Slough just a hundred yards to where the floating buoys marked the location of the traps. Papa Joe leaned over the side while I steadied the boat against the incoming tidal flow. It took a hard pull on the rope to jerk the trap off the muddy bottom and pull it to the surface.

Disappointment. Only one small crab in the first trap. None in the second.

"Well, maybe this isn't a good spot," Papa Joe said. "Maybe the current's too fast here. Let's take these traps up one of the smaller marsh streams out of the way of the big water." We loaded the traps into the bow and headed further north.

We found a mid-sized stream that branched off to the east and coasted slowly with the meandering flow for a couple of turns. The tide was halfway in but still showing the sloping mud banks of the creek. The tidal water would soon flow over the banks and flood the surrounding mud flats. It would cover most of the old tall cordgrass stems and nourish the new growth.

Papa Joe thought there was plenty of depth to cover the traps clear of motors. After placing the traps, we crept slowly and quietly up the stream. When we slid around one curve, Papa Joe signaled to stop the boat. I veered to the right and hit the bank. Both of us grabbed the gunnels to keep from falling off our seats. Papa Joe pointed just a few yards ahead.

"Jack," he whispered, "watch closely right there. See the small waves washing back and forth in front of that mud beach. That's a dolphin making the commotion. He's herding small fish toward the bank and is going to create a wave to push them out of the water."

I got my phone out and started a video.

The dolphin, its tail flukes very visible in the water, came closer and closer to the bank. The last close-in pass pushed water a yard up the sandy bank, and when it drained, several small fish were gasping for air on the bank.

"Watch this!" Papa Joe whispered again. At that moment the eight-foot-long dolphin threw itself almost completely onto the bank and immediately devoured the stranded fish. It flipped back in the water in an instant and was gone. But I caught the rare event on video.

"Wow! That was amazing."

"I've only seen that a few times," Papa Joe said. "It demonstrates how smart these dolphins are. They say the dolphin has the second largest brain compared to its body size of all mammals."

"This video is going up on Instagram tonight! It'll show people how smart dolphins are." I paused a moment, puzzled, "But, who is first?"

"What?"

"First in brain size?

"That would be *us* as a percentage or our bulk," he replied. "But sometimes I think we don't use our smarts as well as the dolphin. We're going to have a hard time beating that example of brain power."

"What hashtag should I give this video?"

Now, Papa Joe was the one with a puzzled look on his face. Finally with a shrug of his shoulders asked, "What's a hashtag?"

I patiently explained, "It's just a label so someone looking for the subject matter might find it. I think I'll hashtag it 'ultimate fisherman.'"

"Oh! How about 'smart dolphins.' I bet a lot of people are looking for dolphins," Papa Joe responded pleased that he understood a new tech tool.

"You got it, Papa Joe."

"That makes sense to me. I guess it's how people of like minds and interests get together. Did you happen to see a fishing line on the dorsal?"

"I'll check the video. No line. Probably not Z-28. Fin markings are very tiny."

We decided this stream would be a good place for the crab traps. Maybe that dolphin knew something we didn't.

We spent the rest of the morning searching other marsh rivers. When we came close to one of the hummocks near high tide, there was enough water under the broad-beamed boat to slip it through the tall marsh grass above the mud flat floor and into the thick cordgrass along the edge.

"Look closely at the stems just above the water," Papa Joe instructed.

"I see them. There are tiny snail-like creatures a few inches above the water. Those critters are smaller than the tip of my little finger. They seem very busy."

"They're the Periwinkle snails your mother loved. They've eaten the algae and plankton deposited on the lower stalk during the last high tide and are waiting for the tide to recede for their next meal," he explained.

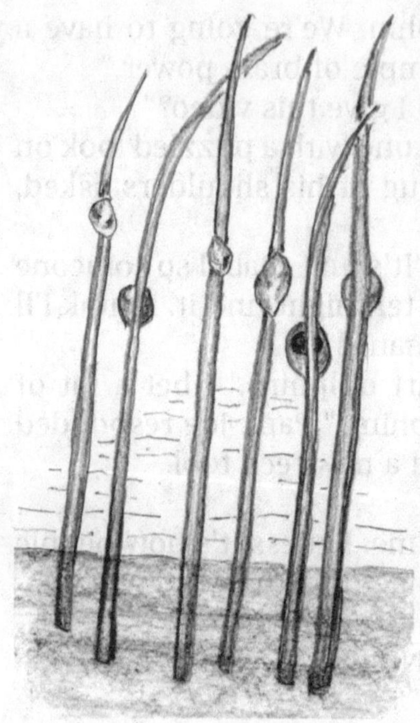

"You'll notice they're well above the water and out of reach of any predators in the water. When the tide goes out, they'll move down the stalk for the new groceries. You could say they have home-delivered meals. The big fish and dolphins aren't going to come through the marsh grass and look for them, but they do provide food for some birds who can crush their shells."

Papa Joe repeated the law of nature: "All the critters and plants here are food supply for someone—even us."

When we motored away from the hummock, the tide had reached its full height for the day. The height of the tide in the Savannah area varied between 7.5 and 9.5 feet. Papa Joe lectured a bit more, "Tides are higher twice a month when the moon is new, and you can't see the low-lying hummocks when it's full. Four times a year the moon is closest to the earth at the full moon, and that's when you get tides that flood low-lying areas. That's when the causeway to Tybee is often under water. It would be devastating to property and cause a great loss of life if a storm hit at the same time as a Harvest moon."

"How's the tide today?" I asked.

"Tonight's a normal full moon, so the tide's a few inches above normal. The highest ever happened two years ago. It measured 10.5 feet by the gauge in the Savannah River at Fort Pulaski. Tide water was over my dock and in my back yard."

"I asked my school friends who went to Destin, Florida for spring break, and they said they hardly noticed the tide. It didn't even take down their sandcastle. How come it's so much bigger here?"

"I asked my dad the same question when I was your age," he admitted. "He said it came from the Atlantic Bight. If you look at a map, from Jacksonville, Florida to the easternmost point of North Carolina, it looks like the Good Lord took a big bite out of the Coast of Georgia and South Carolina," he said with a soft laugh.

"So, when the gravity of the moon pushes against the ocean water there's a smaller place for it to go in the Bight. When you push river water through a canyon, it gets deeper than when it can expand on flat land. How does that sound?"

"Makes sense," I agreed, "but I can see how it could be more complicated when scientists like your friend Willard start explaining."

It was a little after noon when I beached the boat on a small piece of sand on the eastern edge of one of the larger hummocks. "My stomach's telling me it's time for lunch," Papa Joe declared.

"It looks like a lot of people have camped here over the years," I pointed to the edge of a thick forest with a few structures. "That one looks like a full outdoor kitchen complete with a roof and cooking equipment. I thought you were supposed to leave everything the way you found it. That's more than we can tear down with our hammer and crowbar."

"I'm afraid some people have a hard time following the rules. Looks like someone has built facilities for a large group of campers. I'm sure it's nice to use that facility to prepare meals, but structures like this ruin the island's wildness."

"What does Billy say about this?"

"Billy's buddies at DNR have been doing some investigation into who's responsible for this. They aren't happy. Here someone has even cut down trees to make more room for tents and for firewood. All this 'development' takes away the habitat from the wild things the preserve is intended to protect."

"Is DNR going to do something about it?" I persisted.

"Don't know. I know they'd like to find out who did this. Billy says the lower-level staff have asked for money to clear out all this and any other structures they find. So far, no decision from the higher-ups in the agency. They're working on plans which might designate only certain sites for overnight camping. It might mean if you come back next year, we may have to camp in one of the spots DNR designates. I'm hoping they don't make us get a camping permit. The freedom the marsh offers is part of its magic."

"I get that from just two days out here. Do you think this was done by local Tybee people or people from Savannah? Looks like you'd need a big boat to bring all this lumber and cooking equipment here. Must be a big family or someone with lots of friends."

"There are some people on Tybee who know about this, but they're not talking. Some local folks think nobody touches this because the violators have high-up connections to DNR."

"Maybe I should take some pictures. That OK, Papa Joe?"

"Pictures of this would be a good thing."

"Do you still have connections to the *Savannah Morning Post*?"

"No. The people who ran things back in my day are long gone. But I do see where you're going. I wonder if the newspaper knows about this, or if they do, why they're not letting the community hear about it. Sometimes the higher-ups need a little embarrassing article in a newspaper or an online news service to get into action."

"You know we no longer need newspapers to get the word out," I pointed out with a gleeful smile.

"You're right. Let's send Billy the pictures and see what he has to say. He'll probably send them on to his friends at DNR and ask some tough questions. In my day, officials fighting for clean rivers put the polluters on the front page. Maybe we should try to do that today."

"We now have our own front page on Instagram, YouTube, and TikTok. We can be our own reporters," I countered.

"I know you're right, but let's give Billy a chance first."

"Next year will we need a DNR permit to use our site?"

"I don't know. I hope not. They just released a long-term draft plan for this heritage preserve. We'll have to look it up. This marsh *is* the perfect spot to see the variety of vegetation in the maritime forest. They have to do something if people keep eating away at places reserved for wild critters. Let's hope it's not camping permits. We need the freedom and the wilderness."

After lunch we relaxed for a time in the warm sunlight. "Papa Joe, did you, Billy, and Willard really go see the governor?" I asked.

* * * * * *

Papa Joe's Story

Yup, we sure did. My dad also knew about Governor Lester Maddox's Little People's Day. "We certainly fit the description of 'little people,'" my dad said. "So let's go see if he's serious about listening to us ordinary folks." Dad surprised me even more when he said he'd take the day off from his fishing business and drive us to Atlanta.

Dad was my hero, always honest and hardworking, but like other people on the island he was having a hard time making a living from the ocean. His oyster harvesting ended when the Georgia Department of Public Health closed the marsh streams around Tybee after finding too much bacteria in the water and in the oysters. The giant Union Camp paper mill was dumping waste products into the Savannah River, and the City of Savannah was flushing its toilets down the river. I guess they thought it was OK to send the mess out to sea, but at high tide all that polluted water from the river spilled into the marshes. You could say Union Camp put my dad out of business.

Dad still had crab traps he put in the marsh rivers far away from residential development. In shrimping season he pulled some nets with his fishing boat. He knew how to keep old outboard motors running and got some work at the local gas station when people brought their motors in for a tune-up. When I turned twelve, if I got my homework caught up Friday night, I went out with him on Saturdays to help pull the crab traps. I learned how to handle a boat and fish from watching my dad.

Well, we told Mrs. Peabody we had to go to Atlanta to see Governor Maddox and make sure he understood how important Little Tybee was to us. Her delight was written all over her face. She gave us a note for the governor saying this was part of our research project. She instructed us to take careful notes and make a report to the class when we got back. She did make one good suggestion that we first call Dr. Alexander before the trip.

"Hello, this is the UGA Marine Institute."

"This is Willard Elliot from Tybee, and I'd like to speak to Dr. Alexander about saving the Georgia coast."

"I'll transfer you to his office. I just saw him down the hall. I'm sure he'll want to talk with you. He brags on you every day."

Dr. Alexander picked up quickly.

"Dr. Alexander, this is Willard Elliot from Tybee. We're going to follow your suggestion and go see Governor Maddox on his Little People's Day this week. Can you give us some advice?"

"Willard, that's wonderful news," he replied. "There *is* one other thing that might help your argument. I've just come back from Brunswick where I talked with a very smart real estate lawyer who also wants to stop the mining. He admits Kerr-McGee may own the island, but he believes they *don't* own the marsh around it. Georgia is likely under an old law that came to this country from England. Even if the King had given away the dry land to some friend of his, the King still owned all the land the tides cover. According to this lawyer, who's also a member of the legislature, the state got its ownership of the marsh when we had the Revolution and got rid of King George. The new government got the ownership of the marsh from the old English law."

"That's more history than we've learned from Mrs. Peabody, but I'm glad there are smart lawyers on our side of the battle," replied Willard. "We'll tell Governor Maddox he shouldn't be giving our land away."

"I'm sure the governor is a big supporter of private property, so this issue may come up in your conversation. Good luck to you. Send me your paper when you're done. I see a future in science for you."

"We'll let you know how it goes, and if you think of other things we can do, let your friend Mrs. Peabody know."

Back to the governor. My father was not a fan. He didn't understand the governor's earlier actions keeping black folks from eating in his restaurant. That was plain wrong. He grew up working with black people on the shrimp boats and in the fishing industry along the Georgia coast. But he volunteered to drive us to Atlanta to see the governor. My dad knew how important it was for us to do something to save Little Tybee.

Maddox did like to talk. I think that's why he started Little People's Day.

When I walked into the governor's outer office with Willard, Billy, and my dad, it was a little before 11:00 in the morning. That's when the Little People's Day started. The roads to Atlanta weren't so great back then. There was no Interstate 16, so we'd been on the road since 5:00 am. We were all moving a little slowly but perked up when the secretary offered us a

Coca-Cola and peanuts. She said we were the first in line and the governor would be ready to start in about ten minutes.

Dad said we were the talkers and we should go into the office by ourselves. But we said he was the voter and we wanted him to go with us. That turned out to be a good decision.

The governor's office is a pretty big room with his desk at one end and a few chairs at the other end. We noticed he had his bicycle near one of the windows. We'd heard the stories about him riding it backwards around the Capitol.

With a friendly smile, Governor Maddox stepped from behind his desk and invited us to sit. "So, what brings you all the way from Savannah today? That's such a beautiful city." Then he scowled a little, "Why are you three not in school today?"

We handed the governor Mrs. Peabody's note. That cut short the 'stay in school' lecture. The governor read the note carefully with a serious look on his face. "Well, she must be a good teacher. Are you boys good students?" Governor Maddox began. "Wait, don't I remember seeing your pictures in the Savannah papers a couple of weeks back? You're the boys who saved the owner of the Savannah paper. That was a great thing you did. Their reporter Randall Bennett called my press person the next day and wanted to know if there was anything to the mining rumors. I didn't know much about it then but learned more a week later. You kids knew more than the governor," he declared.

"Yes sir," said Willard who was never shy when it was time to talk. "But we don't want to spend our time talking about our grades or saving the publisher." I thought that was a little bold even for Willard. It didn't seem to bother Maddox who could be a little blunt himself.

"Well let's get to it. So, what is the big problem in Savannah?"

"We don't want you to let Kerr-McGee dig up Little Tybee Island and its marshes," Willard stated directly. "It's *our* island. We camp there. We fish there, and lots of people make their living from the marine life that comes from there." I thought that was a good summary even for Willard who sometimes talked a little too much.

"Well," the Governor puzzled a little, "does that mean you own the island and the marsh? I'm a big believer in property rights. I didn't like it when the federal boys told me what to do in my restaurant, and I don't think the government should tell other people what they can do with their property."

"We know you know we don't own the island," Willard said firmly. "We're just kids. Our dads own their homes, but they don't own any islands like some rich folks. That mining company from Texas bought Little Tybee Island from a local businessman. But," getting to his big point with emphasis, "we do own the marsh they want to dig up."

"So, you have a deed that shows you own the marsh?"

"No, we don't. We've done some research and believe the state of Georgia owns the marsh and all the land covered by the tides, and since we are citizens of Georgia, that means we own at least a part of the marsh. We don't want that mining company touching our part of the marsh, and we think those other owners don't want their part to be touched either."

"I can tell you are smart boys, but are any of you lawyers?'

"No. We're not lawyers, at least not yet. Maybe someday," answered Willard a bit pushier than maybe he should have been.

Again, the governor didn't seem to take offense. He said, "I have a lawyer who works for the State of Georgia, called the Attorney General. I've asked him to figure out this part of the issue. But what do you say to all the businesspeople who say this mining project will bring jobs where they're needed?"

Then I spoke up. "My dad needs a good job. The pollution on the coast is taking away many of the jobs that come from the ocean. But, we don't want to wreck our environment to create a job. We camp on the island and fish in the marsh streams and so do many other people. Young people have been educated out there in the ways of Mother Nature for a long time. We care about the dolphins, the birds, and even the hermit crabs who live there."

"So, what does you dad say about the jobs?"

My dad didn't expect to be talking. He usually let others do that and wasn't ready for a question. But he'd been thinking about the issue for some time. To my surprise he spoke right up. "Sir, I work hard with my hands. I have a little business going just like you did. Like most of my friends and like you, I didn't get the education that's now available to these kids. Others know more about the science in this thing and the tax money that might come from a big business like mining, but I think more jobs will come from fishing in a clean ocean and from the tourists who'll come see our beautiful natural coast. I'm with these boys on this one."

"I know you're right about the Savannah River and the other rivers in Georgia," the governor agreed. "We have to clean them up, and I have a good man working on that. His name is Rock Howard, and I like the way he fights for clean water. It's going to take a while, and I'm going to give him the money he needs for the job."

He added, "You'll be pleased to know he's also on your side on this mining proposal."

The governor wound down the session. "Well, I thank you for your advice and for bringing these smart young boys up here to talk to me. I can see they've thought a lot about this. I gotta do a lot of thinking myself. I want to do the right thing for the people of Georgia, and this one's not easy. Lots of people have strong feelings on this here issue."

At that point Billy spoke up. "We thank you for taking time to listen to us. We hope you'll also listen to those smart scientists who live on Sapelo Island. Dr. Alexander told us about the value of the marsh to the sea life on the coast, and we hope you'll hear from him before you decide what's best."

"I like those young researchers. I missed out on all that science as a boy and am very respectful of those who got it. One of my close advisors, George Bagby, is speaking up for the sportsmen in this state who also love the natural areas. They're more interested in hunting in it than looking at, it but they seem to want it to stay as wild as it can be."

The secretary came into the office—our time was more than up. It was OK because we'd made all of our points. We didn't waste any time chit-chatting about the weather or how the newly-arrived Atlanta Braves were doing. The governor seemed to listen to us even though we were just kids.

"Help yourself to a Co-Cola for the road," the governor urged. "If we didn't have other people waiting, I'd give you a ride on my bike. That might get you another picture in the paper. Well, let's take a picture by the bike before you leave. I'll make sure the *Savannah Morning Post* gets a copy and knows you were here."

Feeling good about our talk with the governor,

we slept while Dad drove the long way home. I will always remember my dad for that trip.

Mom met us at the door. Randall Bennett had called and wanted to talk to me about the visit with the governor. He already had the picture and was planning to put it in the paper the next day. I called him back just before his deadline and told him, "It was nice to have the governor of the state listen to three kids. We did notice he didn't tell us what he would finally do but said he would listen to the Attorney General and the scientists. Maybe more people should go to Little People's Day or write him a letter telling him to keep the miners out of our marsh."

I ended the interview with a challenge: "They should ask the governor to 'Save the Coast.'"

* * * * *

91

Chapter 13

Papa Joe looked up and out at the stream. "The water's not moving much right now," he said, "so maybe it's a good time to try the cast net and see what we can catch from the bottom of this small stream. I'll try to show you how, but I have to warn you, I've never been very good at it."

He stood at the edge of the water and demonstrated. "It's generally not a good idea to do this from a boat."

He let the weights attached to the circular net hang straight down from where they attached to the rope and then ran one hand about halfway down the net and looped about a quarter of the circular net over that arm, two weights at a time. He twisted his body back, and in one motion spun around letting the weights spin out on the water in the best circle possible, letting the net sink to the bottom. "That wasn't a very good circle, but maybe it'll catch a few shrimp crawling on the bottom. You pull it in, and let's see what's living down there."

To my delight and Papa Joe's surprise we had five good-sized shrimp in the net and three small minnows. "That was one of my better throws!" he exclaimed. "Must be a lot of adult shrimp right here on their way out to the ocean. Our meal tonight is going to have some variety." We threw the minnows in a bucket with the shrimp in case we might want to try fishing the next day with live bait.

"Jack, you want to try?"

"Sure! But don't expect much."

I followed the instructions. It was a mess the first time. The weights didn't spin out. On the third try I was kind of getting the feel of the throw and got a respectable circle. When I pulled the net in, there were four more shrimp and five minnows.

"That's very, very cool," I said.

Just when I was about to throw again, we heard the whine of what seemed like a big outboard motor. It wasn't long before a 25-foot shiny Yamaha fishing boat pulled up on the sand and a mature German Shepherd bounded onto the sand followed by a young guy who secured the boat with an anchor in the sand. The dog went right to me. Sniffed my feet. I offered the back of a nervous hand.

"Don't worry about my dog, he's very friendly," the blond, tanned, young man said in a friendly voice.

"Hey, how is the fishing this afternoon?"

"We're just trying out this cast net. Not much good at it, but we did get a few decent-sized shrimp that were passing by. What brings you out here in the middle of the day?" Papa Joe asked. We could see the six-foot-something broad-shouldered young dude didn't have any fishing gear in the boat. He was wearing flip flops. It was unlikely he was here to fish or gather oysters, but there were four large coolers in the boat.

"My dad sent me out here to get ready for the gathering planned for tonight. A few of his law firm partners are bringing their families here for a seafood boil. Since it's spring break, the kids can stay out a little late. I'm here to get things ready. Love this place. Don't you?"

"Do you know...," I started when Papa Joe gave me a little negative shake of his head and interrupted.

"Nice facilities you have here. You help your dad build this?" As he spoke, he looked at me and then looked down and touched his phone. I got the message. While looking straight at our visitor, my fingers flew across the buttons on my phone.

"Dad and a few of his friends have been working at this for a couple of years. My friends and I helped. I love working in the sun and then diving into the water to cool off. In high school we've had some nice parties here, and a few of my college friends are coming in on Saturday for a get-together. Some of us are planning to stay over."

Trying to keep the conversation going, Papa Joe said "You look like maybe you play a little football. I did that in my day."

"Yeah, in high school. I'm at UGA now and not good enough for that competition."

"How does everybody get here?" Papa Joe continued probing.

"They'll come on a couple of boats from the marina on Wilmington Island. It only takes about ten minutes. Are you guys doing any camping? You could certainly use this spot. We don't own it, and anyone can come here and use what we've built. It's a great place where dogs can run free."

I noticed the German Shepherd. bored with the conversation, had taken off into the wooded area of the hummock.

"Thanks for the invite. We've got a nice spot at the end of Little Tybee and probably should be getting back to see what the high tide might have done to our gear. We're hoping to see some more dolphin and catch a few fish for dinner in the outgoing tide."

"I love that camping spot. My dog also likes to run free on the sand bars just south of where the Slough empties. Lots of interesting birds down there."

"Nice meeting you," I said, trying to be polite. "How about a picture?" I said with an unreadable face.

"Glad to oblige."

I got a close-up of the young man standing in front of the facilities and slipped my phone back into my pocket as we packed up to leave.

"The weights on that cast net are heavy. Maybe we could try it again near our campsite," I said as I put the net, the bucket, and the leftovers from lunch into the bow of the boat.

As Papa Joe pushed off, he said, "Glad you had the chance to try it out. I think you're a natural. Outdoor living will get you in better shape before you know you're doing anything different."

"Enjoy your gathering tonight." he hollered to the young man.

With the young man unloading his boat in the distance, I checked my phone to see what I'd captured. The still shots of the facilities were clear, and the young man in front of them could be easily identified. The video was shaky, and its first frames started with sand and flip flops. It had a very odd upward angle, and the young man went in and out of view, but there was a clear recording of him talking about building the extensive facilities and the parties they had there. "This looks like evidence to me. What do we do with it? Should I post it?" I asked eagerly.

"We send it to Billy and get his advice. He has been an intimate part of DNR politics for a lifetime, and I trust his judgment better than my own. It would be interesting if DNR enforcement would do a little drop-in at the party tonight."

Papa Joe checked the position of the sun in the western sky and concluded, "It's probably time to go back to the campsite and start cooking our dinner. This has been a pretty full day. I'm also kinda interested to see how far this full-moon tide came up at our campsite. Sea rise threatens a lot of coastal property, even our secure campsite."

We went south at trolling speed with eyes out for the great birds of the marsh. I again manned the motor. After a few moments of slow cruising, Papa Joe, who was sitting in the bow, pointed to the east to some tall trees on one of the larger hummocks.

"There. That's a colony of egrets. They've been searching for food all day and are starting to come back to their nests. They're part of a group of wading birds who stalk their prey in the marsh grass. Beautiful, but lethal. They stand motionless in the marsh grass patiently waiting for an unsuspecting meal to wander by. Then they use their big weapon. Their slender neck coils like some snakes, and they thrust a long sharp beak into their prey."

"Look there!" I said excitedly. A tall gray bird stood completely still above the cordgrass.

"Go a little closer."

As I angled the boat closer to the cordgrass, the gray-blue bird, sensing human presence, stretched its wings and jumped into the air. It was majestic. Its wingspan was nearly equal to its height, and after only two effortless pushes from its wings, it glided calmly over the marsh grass and landed in the marsh out of reach, but not out of sight.

"That's a Great Blue Heron, king of the waders," Papa Joe said with admiration. "Those birds are often four feet in height with a wingspan to match. They love this environment. Lots of easy pickings."

"I'd love for you to see another Bald Eagle. An impressive bird. They're very different from the waders. I'd like you to see them dive on a fish, and without landing, pull their prey out of the water with their piercing talons, and just keep flying back to their nest."

At the campsite, the tide had crept to the edge of the fire ring, but our possessions were high and dry. We re-lit the campfire and got a good blaze going so when it died down there would be a bed of coals for cooking.

I got out my phone and wrote a text to Jane Olmstead. "We were up and down the Slough today, but no sightings."

While we were waiting for the pot of water for the shrimp to boil, my phone buzzed.

"Jack, this is Billy. Are you sitting down?"

"Do you have dolphin news?"

"Yes, I do, young man, and I think you're going to find it very interesting. Day after tomorrow, a team from DNR, NOAA, and maybe a dolphin expert from Sea World are going to attempt a rescue of your dolphin. They want to get the fishing line off its dorsal fin before it can do any more damage. From the markings on her dorsal fin they know for sure she's Z-28."

"Wow! That's a quick response. When? Where? And can we be a part of it?"

"They say yes, you can come along. Watch mainly, but maybe help. Tomorrow they again want you to look out for her so they can focus the search when the team comes together. They'll come into the marsh near your campsite the next day."

I put my phone on speaker so Papa Joe could get into the conversation. "Where can we meet them?" he asked.

"They know where your campsite is, and they'll meet you there mid-morning. Probably 10:30. The high tide is at 12:30, and that'll give four hours for search and rescue and still have plenty of water to get back out to the ocean. Their boats sit deeper in the water than your Johnboat, so two to three hours after high tide the water gets too shallow for them to get out past the sandbars near your camp. They know Z-28's history and should find her in the Tybee Slough. When they show up, they'll detail a plan."

"We'll be ready. We'll be more than ready," we both said at the same time.

"What about our young friend and his wilderness dining facilities?"

"You two are certainly building a great adventure. DNR needs more eyes and ears like yours. I sent the pictures and the video to an enforcement friend I worked with. I'm sure he knows about the site but doesn't know what the higher-ups are planning to do about it. Over his pay grade, he says. Maybe your video will make it harder for them to ignore."

"How about a little pressure from social media?" I asked. "I think I could manage that."

"You're tough ..., and right. It often takes some public pressure to give government the backbone to act. Maybe post the pictures of the facility with a comment but hold off on the pictures of the young man. He's not an innocent, but maybe the world created by social media shouldn't fall on him. The existence of the video might encourage his father to negotiate with DNR. I don't want you in the middle of a legal mess. No telling what a den of lawyers can and will do to protect their interest or a son."

"Sounds like good advice. I've seen myself how social media can be a pretty nasty place. It would be nice if the video was enough of a threat to get some action out of DNR to stop the violators of the wild."

"Jack, where do you plan to put the pics of the restaurant facility? I'll send it on to my few followers."

"I'll put it on Instagram with hashtags: #Little Tybee or #Preserve Violators or #Marsh Restaurant."

"There's a private Tybee residents' Facebook

page. I'm a member, so I'll re-post it there with a comment. Locals follow that site. I'm sure a few residents know and use the site, but everybody else is not going to be happy a few fat cats are taking advantage of the wild.

"You two have some busy and exciting days ahead. I wish I could be there with you, but I have to stay close to home. My wife had some flu symptoms this morning. Besides, a crowd's not good for a stressed dolphin."

"Thanks for doing this Mr. Wagner. Glad you still have those DNR connections. I hope your wife is OK."

"Keep in touch," Billy said and hung up.

I looked at Papa Joe to see what he thought of Billy's advice. "He has more experience dealing with the ins and outs of politics. I'm not afraid of a battle, but sometimes a little subtlety is a good thing. Being on the front page of the *Savannah Morning Post* may alter a person's behavior. That was very effective back in my day.

"Time to focus on the rescue. It's going to be very interesting. In all my years out here I've never had a chance to see the pros take on a task like this. But right now I think we better be cooking this great seafood feast that's in front of us."

The meal was a delight. Fish fillets cooked on a little grill over the coals, boiled shrimp, and some roasted red potatoes. We even had some cocktail sauce Papa Joe had thrown into the bottom of the cooler.

I turned to the outdoor chef, "That was wonderful! How did you learn to cook like that?" Then I added jokingly, "Maybe some ice cream next time?"

"Your grandmother Mary was a wonderful cook, especially when it came to seafood. I'd watch her closely in the kitchen. Occasionally, with very specific directions, she let me cut a few things up. But when

Mary and I went camping in the wilderness, I was the guy who cooked. I also learned a lot by trial and error with Billy and Willard on our camping adventures. We did have some burned food," he admitted.

"You guys had a lot of adventures," I noted. "I think we're going to have a few of our own before we go back to civilization."

Jack

Chapter 14

Just as I got out of my tent in the gray light of a new day, my phone buzzed. "Jack, this is Jane Olmstead from NOAA. Sorry to wake you so early."

"No problem. I'm up."

"We're organizing a rescue team for Z-28. Our veterinarian has reviewed your great photos and concluded the polymer fishing line *is* life threatening and must come off immediately. Our team will rendezvous at your location about two hours before high tide tomorrow. Dr. Jason Landon of DNR will be the team leader. He'll have five boats with two people per boat. We've been able to put together a very experienced team with members from South Carolina, Georgia, and North Florida. We'll have a mammal veterinarian with us."

"Wow that's exciting! Can we help?" I asked, now fully awake.

"Yes, you can." Jane Olmstead assured me.

"The first phase of the operation is the search. If you could survey the Tybee Slough today, it might help us locate her tomorrow. She doesn't have a satellite tag, so your information will be critical to our success. When he arrives, Jason will give you one of our VHF radios so you can communicate with the other boats when we search tomorrow. It sometimes takes two hours to locate a dolphin, but the locations you give us should shorten that search.

"The next task is to find a safe place to attempt the rescue. Jason will explain more when he arrives.

101

There's a lot of risk here for both the humans and Z-28."

"Do we get to help with the actual rescue?"

"Sorry, no. That's tough work," Jane replied. "Team members need 'hands-on experience' with a dolphin before we would ever put them in this situation. But since you're so good with your phone, some video of the final phase would be great. People need to see the harm some simple fishing line or wire mesh can do, and they need to know how much we care about every single one of these beautiful creatures."

"Thanks for letting us be part of this. I'll do the best I can with the video."

"Thanks for all you've done so far, Jack. I hope you're having a great time out there with your granddad. The marsh is a beautiful but dangerous place, and you're getting a VIP education."

Jane hung up with encouragement, "Good luck in your search today."

"So, what's the word?" Papa Joe asked as he stretched his back before moving too far from his tent.

I turned to him excitedly. "The rescue is on for tomorrow!" I said with a broad smile. "This is going to be a very big deal—five boats and a ten-person team. She said we can help today by locating where Z-28 likes to hang out."

"She's probably at the north end of the Slough where we spotted her last time," grandfather mused aloud. "But she could've gone south toward Williamson Island with the high tide. Since we have all day, let's check south while the tide is going out and then search north this afternoon. That'll give me a chance to show you a bit of the wildlife on the remote sand bars and oyster reefs there.

"Here's a little quiz for you," Papa Joe posed, "Have you ever heard of the Atlantic Flyway?"

"Flyway? Is that where the Air Force pilots learn to fly their jets?"

Papa Joe raised an eyebrow and knitted his forehead in response, "There *are* many military jet pilots practicing in the remote parts of the coast. But no, these wings are attached to bird bodies."

He went into teaching mode. "The Flyway is a trail along the coast from the Caribbean to Greenland. Some birds travel even further, from South America into the Arctic. This island is a stopover for those birds flying north or south in the spring and fall migrations. More than 20 different species use this area as a grocery store to eat and pack in food for the next leg of their trip. Without these wild islands and the tidal sand bars and mud flats many of these birds wouldn't make it home."

"I've never done much bird watching," I admitted. "But it might be interesting to see what they're doing early in the morning. I bet they're looking for breakfast. I was thinking about that myself."

"I'd like to get going quickly so we see things in the early light. How about a piece of bread smeared with peanut butter for now and we can come back for more in a couple of hours? Would that feed the dragon?"

"It might keep it at bay a little. I'm game for a *quick* look."

Bread in hand, we jumped into the boat. Adjusting to the low tide, Papa Joe had to change the angle and depth of the motor, and the bottom scraped a little sand as it slid through the shallow channel at the end of the island and out into the calm ocean.

"That move shows the advantage of this small flat boat," Papa Joe pointed out. "It's perfect for shallow water but doesn't like rough water."

Soon we were beaching the boat on the shore side

of a mud-flat island. The mud was drying in the morning sun on the bit of earth that appeared only at low tide. It was too shallow for the boat to pass between the mud island and the sandy beach, but a great place to view the birds prowling for food. Some birds rested facing into the breeze from the northeast.

"Do you think we'll see a skimmer?" I asked, remembering my mother's favorite bird.

"Maybe. They usually fish at night along the edges of streams, but I have seen them in the early hours and at dusk. It's fun to watch their technique. They usually make two passes, one to make a line on the surface which attracts small fish and a second to snag those that got too curious.

"This area is great for traveling birds, especially this time of the year," Papa Joe lectured. "It's the spawning season for the Horseshoe Crabs, and the females are dropping lots of high-protein eggs on the sand every night. One female can drop as many as 120,000 eggs, so we're talking about a feast for the bird population."

My eyes opened wide, "Whoa, that's a lot of eggs!"

"See all those six- to eight-inch shells?" Papa Joe indicated with a sweep of his hand. "The shells don't mean dead animals. These crabs shed their shells sixteen times during their life. It takes ten years from the day a newborn Horseshoe Crab hatches, before they come back here to create some little ones. Scientists call them a keystone species—a lot of other animals depend on 'em.

"The funny thing is," he continued, "Horseshoe Crabs are really a part of the spider family, been around more than 300 million years."

"That means even before the dinosaurs, I declared.

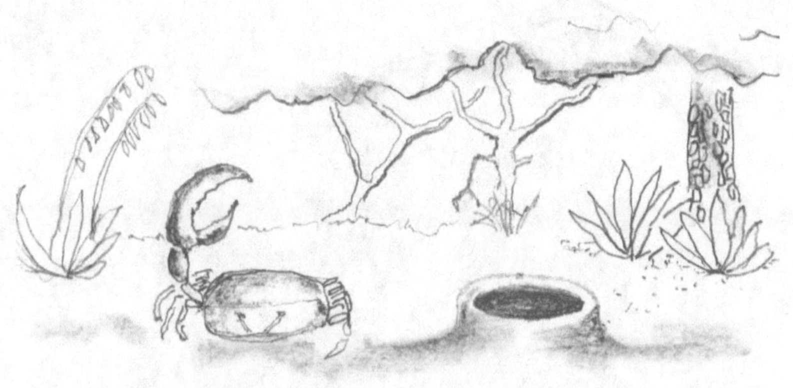

"What about these little guys?" I asked, pointing to the edge of the mud flat.

"That's a Fiddler Crab," he chuckled. It's a real part of the crab family. They're tiny, and millions live in little holes in the mud along this coast. When they come out of their burrows at low tide, the fast birds like the sandpipers and plovers can run them down before they get back to safety."

I spotted one with only one claw. "Do you think it was injured?"

"No," he said with a wide smile, "that one's a male, and he's waving that rather useless claw to lure a female into his burrow. His mate will have two claws so she can push more food into her body and produce more little ones. He's hoping to make some babies when he mixes it up with a female at the bottom of his burrow."

The more I looked around, the more I noticed the wildlife around me, "That bird on the muddy bank with a long bill that curves down—what's it called?"

"That's a Whimbrel. There are a lot of them here this time of the year. They're amazing creatures. A few will nest here for the summer and raise young ones,

but the Whimbrel's a long-distance traveler. It like-ly flew here directly from South America and is now busy loading up on food for a long flight to the Arctic in a couple of weeks. Sometimes it'll fly 2500 miles over open water."

"That's pretty cool. But why does it have that long beak?"

"It's looking closely at the tiny piles of mud balls. When there are no easy Horseshoe Crab eggs to be found, it'll look for its second favorite meal, the Fid-dler Crab."

"They look too small for us to eat," I said. "It would take a lot of 'em to make a meal."

"But they're the perfect food for the Whimbrel. It catches them running for home, or it can thrust that backward curved beak down into a burrow and drag one out."

"So those crabs can run, but they can't hide. I think it got one," I pointed out excitedly Look, it's shaking it—it tore the claws off. Oh man, it swallowed the rest whole."

"It doesn't like the claws but somehow digests the rest of it."

Papa Joe directed my attention toward the beach side of the mud flat. "That's a beginning oyster bed, and it's the perfect food mart for the American Oyster Catcher—big birds—up to 20 inches long with a 30-inch wingspan. They  have a unique bill too. It's half the length of the Whimbrel's and laterally flat at the end."

"How does it get those boogery oysters out of their shells?"

"That's one smart bird with a plan. It walks on the bed when the water is just covering the oysters. Their shells are open, bringing in and spitting out water. The Oyster Catcher uses its bill like a sword and thrusts between the open shells to cut the abductor muscle. It has to get a clean cut before the oyster uses the muscle to snap shut. If it misses the muscle, the oyster will hang onto the bird's bill until one or the other dies."

"Ooh! That's harsh."

"Sometimes you're the feeder, and sometimes you're the food. A little darkness seems to come with every bit of beauty out here."

Papa Joe hesitated but couldn't resist another teaching moment. Once a tour guide, always a tour guide. "Let's move over to the little sandy beach to see if we can find some nests. These little sandbars are perfect nesting grounds for small birds."

We walked along a line of dead decaying cordgrass left on the sand from the last tide. "That little structure with a few green plants growing is called marsh wrack. Over time it'll catch more sand and build into a dune if not blown away by a storm. It's also a great nesting place above the tide. Birds like the Wilson's Plover, the Oyster Catcher, and smaller Sandpipers just push the sand aside and make a hollow place to lay their eggs. Parents have to sit on the nest to keep them warm or cool. On a hot day and in direct sun, the eggs can cook, and the young hatchlings can't regulate their own temperature and would die in a matter of minutes. The parents provide the shade the tiny ones need right after hatching."

A small squawking bird flew just over their heads. "What's up with that guy?" I asked involuntarily ducking.

"I bet that's a protective parent. We must be close to a nest. His or her mate is on the nest, and it's telling us to get lost. Let's not go closer. Here are the binoculars so you can look from a distance. See if you can spot a bird resting in the marsh wrack."

"I see it! It looks about eight inches long with brown wings. It's almost the color of the sand."

"It could be a Wilson's Plover. This is where they like to nest. It's harder and harder for them to find a place where people and their dogs don't disturb them. Let's back away. The wildlife people from DNR actually ask us not to walk above the line of the latest tide. You can see why."

When we turned to walk back to the boat, I almost stepped on a tiny fluffy object. A young hatchling lay dead on the sand just below the last tide line.

"Oh no," moaned Papa Joe, "just what we were talking about."

"Look here," I said, pointing to an area just below the tide line. "There's a dog paw print here and not a little dog."

"Could be another wild animal or," Papa Joe hesitated, "it could be a German Shepherd. These are some big animal footprints."

"And look," I pointed, "there are more prints just above where the high tide came yesterday. I think someone let their dog run free out here last evening. Do we know anyone like that?"

"We do. And look at the other print. This looks like it was made by a large-sized flip-flop. I think our young city man came down here and let his dog run free, and this dead hatchling is the result. One less shore bird to join the Atlantic Flyway. Get that camera out and capture some evidence. We'll also make sure DNR has an opportunity to examine this little dead creature."

"You know, we do have some pictures in my phone of flip-flops on large feet," I stated emphatically.

"We'll use Billy to get all this in front of the right people at DNR and let them decide what to do with it. I'm not sure if laws have been broken, but this shows someone has ignored DNR's advice."

"There should be a law," I said, as I went about capturing the prints and the nearby frail carcass. I felt like a crime scene photographer.

When we were done with the "crime scene," Papa

Joe had one more warning for me. "Keep your eyes open on the back side of the sandbar. It's a sunny spot out of the wind and Timber Rattlers like to sun themselves on the warm sand."

"Oooh—you don't have to say that twice."

"Gotta have both sides of nature in your head out here, danger and delight."

I'd gotten used to the little bits of information coming from my Papa Joe. Not really a lecture.

Back in the boat, we cruised slowly south along the marsh and dunes of Williamson Island and up a small inlet.

"If I was a dolphin, I'd hang out in the marsh rivers of this new and isolated island," Papa Joe said. "It's not traditionally recognized as one of Georgia's barrier islands, but the view east goes all the way to England, so I think it qualifies."

But no sign of Z-28 in this area. The tide was starting to flood the Slough and the marsh of Little Tybee, so we headed back to camp.

"I'm ready for that late breakfast you promised."

Brunch was last night's leftovers of fried fish and two blackened potatoes we'd cooked in the coals. Under Papa Joe's watchful eye, I scrambled some eggs to add to the leftovers.

"Tasty," I said as I leaned back in the sand. "Do you think we have a little time to finish your saving Little Tybee story?" I peppered Papa Joe with lots of questions. "In your fight to save Little Tybee did you, Willard, and Billy go to that hearing in Savannah? Did you have some reinforcements in your fight to save Little Tybee? I'm curious." I persisted. "So what happened next? When did they decide this thing?"

"Not for a while yet, Jack. Government responds slowly. It takes a lot of people and a lot of patience to make it move to your direction."

* * * * *

Papa Joe's Story

The hearing in Savannah was long. Attorney General Bolton decided to let everyone talk, and lots of people wanted to talk. At first it was held in a community room at the headquarters of Savannah Power and Light. We got there early and sat a few rows behind all the government officials. "The Suits," as Billy called them, looked very, very official in dark suits and ties. The meeting room filled up quickly, and soon it was standing room only.

Soon some important-looking guy told us, "Move to the back boys and give your seats to adults." We didn't like it much, but we did. By the end of the day, we were sitting on the floor in the back of the room.

Dr. Alexander was there. He was a little more scientific than when he talked at school, but his main point was the same. When measuring all the nutrients coming off the marsh, "it was the most productive farmland per acre in the United States and probably in the world."

A person from an organization called the Sierra Club stated their opposition. I had never heard of this club. He said they had members all over the country and had just started a club here in Georgia. Most of their members were graduate students from the University of Georgia doing research on the oceans and marshlands.

One man said he didn't want the marsh disturbed because when he was rowing his girlfriend through the marsh he tried to get his first kiss. His girlfriend said, "This is the wrong place and the wrong time." That got a nice laugh from the crowd. "Well," he said, "This mining proposal is in the wrong place, and it's the wrong time." The people of Savannah, he said, would be stuck with the problem while the folks in Atlanta were counting their money. He never did say if he got his first kiss.

Another man stood up with a warning. Nobody should be digging around in the marsh because in 1958 the U. S. Air Force accidentally dropped an atomic bomb somewhere near Tybee, and they might just find it with one of the giant earth-moving machines Kerr-McGee would be using. The audience gasped. We looked at each other, not sure if there really was a live bomb in our marsh.

A big man, about 6'4" strode to the podium and gripped it with large, strong hands. Somebody whispered that he had grown up in Savannah and had been a boxing champ in college and in the Navy. You could see that just by looking at him. He was Rock Howard, the state official Governor Maddox said was responsible for keeping rivers clean. He declared the company had not given him a plan and stated loudly and clearly that without a lot of careful engineering work they were not getting a permit from him.

"Yeah!" we silently mouthed, throwing our fists in the air.

The most fun speaker was the Fish and Game guy named George Bagby. He was a very short round man, but maybe not as round as Round Man. They had to bring the mike way down so he could reach it. Governor Maddox had put him in charge of the land the state of Georgia owned for hunting and fishing. His friends in the legislature liked to call him the "Fish Head."

For a little guy, he sure could get people riled up against mining the marsh. He argued the deal would give away Georgia's future for a tiny cash payment.

Just like my dad, he said the future of the coast was tourism and the fishing industry. "No one's going to get off the new Interstate 95 to look at a phosphate mine, and no one's gonna buy a beach house with murky brown water left from dredging the marsh." I was proud my dad had told Governor Maddox the same thing.

George Bagby said the price Kerr-McGee offered for all the acres was way low and it looked like the worst deal since the Yazoo Land Fraud in early Georgia history. We didn't know what that was, but I knew not to tell Mrs. Peabody about that part of the speech. That sounded like another one of her written reports.

Well, the hearing went on all day, and there were still more people who wanted to talk. Arthur Bolton was true to his word—he wanted to hear from everybody. So, he moved the hearing to the Hilton Ballroom the next day so everybody could get into the room. Our get-out-of-school-free card was only good for one day, but we came back anyway. We found out you had to sign up in order to speak. Willard had the nerve to speak and was number 25 on the list to talk the second day.

We'd worked up a little speech the night before, but when Willard got up in front of all those people in suits and ties, he couldn't read our science arguments. It didn't matter. Willard just talked about our camping and fishing expeditions in the marsh. The best part was when he talked about the dolphins we knew. "Why," he asked, "would anyone dig up this marsh where kids could go and get to know a dolphin family?" Everybody listened to this sincere, studious 13-year-old kid. When he sat down there was applause.

Over the two days 200 people talked. I think only two said anything good about the proposal, and one was the architect the company had hired to show some sketches of what the land would look like when they were done.

When the day was almost over, Billy elbowed me. "Look at the front row where speakers are getting ready to talk. Who do you see?"

Not being as tall as Willard or Billy, I half stood up and looked closely. There in the front row was Commissioner White next in line to talk. I whispered, "Do you think he's going to go against what all these other people have said?"

"I bet you a dollar he doesn't," said Billy.

Fortunately for me I didn't take that bet. He was right. Commissioner White said he had changed his mind about the mining of the marsh. "I started thinking about the project when a 7th-grader from Tybee School came to see me. He's that smart young man who talked here this morning. I confess I didn't understand the longer-term value of the marsh, which the scientists have explained, and now I see we cannot let Kerr-McGee destroy what nature has created. You know I do a little real estate, and I think I'll sell more properties looking out on the marsh than looking at huge earth-moving equipment. I'm going to write the governor and tell him to turn this deal down."

"Wow," Willard whispered, "I think we helped get another vote for our side."

"Do you think it was us, the scientists, or the size of this crowd?" I asked. "That guy knows how to put his finger in the air and tell which way the wind is blowing. I think we've gone from a little breeze to a real Nor'easter."

Sometimes I think those two days were better than going to college. We knew a lot more about mining and about that new term, ecology. It meant the plants and animals, big and tiny, were in one big system and their interaction kept the whole thing together. The ocean was a big system, and all of its parts had to work together or it would fall apart.

I think that public hearing was the reason Willard became an environmental scientist.

"So that's the end of the story?" I asked.

"No, not quite. Getting solutions takes time. The whole story is probably not even done today."

How can that be? I wondered.

* * * * * *

Jack

Chapter 15

Papa Joe and I both sensed our free time in the marsh together was getting near the end. Tomorrow after the rescue we'd have to go back to Tybee for supplies, a charge, and gas if we were going to spend another day in the marsh. Or maybe water skiing.

"There's one more bird I wish you could see: The long-flying Red Knot."

"Let's go find it!" I replied with enthusiasm that surprised him just a little.

"We can't do it right now; we have a job to do. But during the most recent DNR bird count they found a large flock of nearly 2000 on the two little islands along the south bank of the main Savannah River channel."

"What makes this bird so special?" I asked.

"It's another long-distance flyer, but a bit smaller than the Whimbrel—about the size of a large robin. It even looks a little like a robin. It starts its flight from the very tip of South America. Then it loads up on food here and, like most of the other long-haulers, flies non-stop to the Arctic Circle. The total trip is 9000 miles."

"Wow! That's some trip. Maybe after the rescue and after we get resupplied, we could venture out into the Savannah River."

"We could try. Have to check the river traffic. Those ocean freighters headed for the Savannah port push a lot of water around, and we would need to avoid them and stay away from their wakes."

I made sure the binoculars were handy and checked the power bars on our phones. I used my battery storage device for a third charge on mine. Maybe one more good charge left or part of one. We turned the phones off to save the juice for when it would be needed.

All afternoon I was at the tiller as we slowly cruised north and south on the Slough with side trips into the largest tributary creeks.

"Maybe we should try to find the nest of that eagle we saw on the beach the other day," I suggested. "I'd like to see if there are babies."

"They're called chicks, eaglets, or fledglings when very young, and later nestlings or juveniles," said Papa Joe in what I imagined was his tour guide voice.

I guided the boat past our campsite and followed the narrow creek on the back edge of the large island. Papa Joe signaled for me to cut the motor. He aimed his binoculars at the high branches of a mature pine tree and focused on a large clump of sticks and mud.

"This is one of the two nests here. An eagle pair comes back to this nest every year. They nest in the winter, so if they've been successful, we should see some mature juveniles," he said, handing me the binoculars.

"There are two peeking over the edge," I whispered. "They're big. Must have been a good year. We should let the DNR people know."

"I'm sure they know about these two additions to our slowly growing coastal count."

"Let's make one more try up at the north end of the Slough to find our friendly dolphin," I suggested, handing the binoculars back. I was determined to find Z-28. "Maybe after looking, we might check if any crabs found our trap and also do a little fishing for our dinner."

118

"Sounds like a plan."

We went north on the Slough at a little past high tide and followed a marsh river that came very close to the Tybee Causeway. Still no sign of our dolphin. Then, turning south we reached the start of the large deep river that flowed west toward Savannah. Here a fin broke the surface.

"This could be it," I yelled, over the sound of the outboard.

Papa Joe had his binoculars on the fin. "I think it looks like Z-28. She's moving south on the Slough."

When we caught up to her, we were sure. I turned on my phone and sent a picture to Jane Olmstead with a message. "We spotted her at the north end after a lot of searching. She seems to like the north end of the island at high tide."

"Great work," she texted back "This will help Jason a lot tomorrow. Let her go her way for now."

On our way to home base we checked the crab traps. Success! Five large blue crabs would be a nice addition to our meal.

While Papa Joe got the fire going, I caught two trout—adding to our meager dinner. We heated our last can of baked beans in a pan on the open fire. It was enough. We had stretched two days of supplies into four by living off the land, but basics were nearly gone. We did have marshmallows cooked over the fire to top off the meal.

The fire burned down. After producing a spectacular show, the sunset dissolved into dark over the western rim of the marsh. Papa Joe asked, "Was this an OK day?"

"Yes. Not as exciting as the other days, but good," I assured him. "There always seems to be something new to see and explore. Those birds sitting on a nest are hard to see. Their color blends with the sand and keeps them safe. The fierce little guy that flew at us was cool. I learned a lot and made some memories to think about."

"Everything out here needs some form of protection if it's going to survive. Color is a big part of the defense. The skimmer's little tricky line in the water may seem simple, but without it those birds might not survive."

I hesitated a moment but ventured, "Maybe I'm ready for a restaurant."

"Oh, you're done with my cooking?" Papa Joe asked with a smile.

"No, I love it. The fish is wonderful—but maybe not every night. That's why we have restaurants. Don't people say variety is the spice of life?"

"Plenty of variety out here, but I know you can't find a pizza," Papa Joe admitted with full understanding.

"The other thing people like about restaurants is you don't have to make the food, and you don't have to clean up after you eat it."

"You're right, Jack. I like that too. There are some decent restaurants on Tybee."

"I know. We went to a good one. I liked A-J's even though I was still punishing mom for making me come here."

"Did she make the right decision?"

"Absolutely! This has been sick, and it's not even over."

"I'm glad. I love this place."

As we were about to go to our tents, I noticed some movement in the top of the live oak above our campsite. "I think there's a little bird up there."

Just then a dramatic flash of color swooped down and perched on a branch just over our heads. "Wow! Look at those colors— bright red, blue, and green." I said with delight brimming from my voice.

"*That* is a Painted Bunting. It's the most dramatic songbird in the wooded part of the island. I think it knew we were looking at birds most of the day and wanted to show off a little. It's rare to see one out here."

"Nice way to end the day," I said. "This day has had a nice rhythm, a little slow and gentle. And I like the company." I gave Papa Joe a reassuring grin. "Tomorrow is going to be very different."

Jack

Chapter 16

The twenty-foot double-hulled boat with NOAA Fisheries in bright green lettering on its shiny white hull cut through the inlet and pulled into our creek just as we finished cleaning the campsite and packing a lunch. Four other boats idled in the middle of the Slough.

"You must be Jack," said the broad-shouldered man in the front of the boat. He was well-tanned from days and years in coastal waters and spoke with a slow, soft southern drawl. "I'm Jason, and I'll be trying to lead these ruffians today. I think we're going to do a great thing today thanks to you and your grandpa."

Jason continued his introduction, "I'm a biologist focused on sea mammals for the Coastal Division of Georgia's Department of Natural Resources. We've got help from the NOAA division office and South Carolina Fish and Wildlife, plus a veterinarian from Sea World."

"We're ready to take your directions," Papa Joe said. "Tell us if we're getting in the way. We've spotted Z-28 a couple of times just before Jack's Cut comes into the Slough near the big marsh river that goes toward Savannah, but I'm sure she knows all the little creeks off the Slough."

"We'll start in the northern creeks and move south. Here's your radio so you can keep track of the creeks the other boats are covering. Your understanding of this marsh is going to be very helpful." I was standing in the bow, and Jason handed me a compact radio. Papa Joe was at the motor.

"What happens if we spot her?" I asked.

"First take a close-up picture of her fin and send it to me. We'll need to be sure it's her." We exchanged cell numbers.

"After sighting, we'll probably be following her around the marsh for a while so we can find the right location for the capture. We don't want any oyster reefs around that might cut her or us. We need three to five feet of water so our guys can stand in the water and get their arms around her. She might go to the bottom, and then we'll need to lift her out of the water so she can breathe through her blowhole."

"How do you catch her?"

Jason pointed to the net in the front of his boat. "We need to get this circled around her before we get in the water. We can draw the net closer in. When she noses into the net, four of us will move in quickly and get our arms around her. She generally likes humans, but she's not going to want us to be so personal, so we'll make it as quick as possible."

"You and your grandpa stay clear of that final operation. Use your phone to document this. I hear you're pretty good with that. All of us would love to have some good video when we're done."

Jason threw his arm in a circle in the air as a signal, "Let's go find us a dolphin!"

In single file they motored slowly north on the wide slough with eyes on the narrow creeks along the way. The sun glared off the calm water. A few small fish broke the surface, but it was a quiet moment despite the whirring of the outboards at quarter throttle. North of the Cut they split up to survey the streams which came from many different directions.

The radio popped. "We're close to the causeway, and no fins sighted."

Another radio. "We're close to the intracoastal and turning back."

Papa Joe and I had gone north along a narrow, developed upland spit attached to Tybee Island, but we saw nothing.

"Turn back south and check all the tributary creeks on either side," Jason instructed over the radio.

When Papa Joe and I reached the area near the Cut, a small fin broke the water about thirty feet in front of us. It was moving toward the Slough. In a moment two other larger fins broke the surface and the small one was in between them. All three were moving in the same direction.

I quickly mashed the radio, "We have a sighting of a small pod moving toward the Slough near the start of the Cut."

"Again. What direction are they headed? Over." asked Jason.

"Looks like they're heading south from here. Over."

"Get a little closer and see if you can send me a picture of the largest dorsal fin," replied Jason.

"I'm sending you what I have, and we'll try to move up." Papa Joe powered up the engine but stayed out of the path of the dolphins.

"I think that's her" I whispered.

"Looks like her fin markings."

I clicked the radio on, "Sending you a picture. Can't see the line, but we think it's her. She looks the same size, and the fin looks the same. Over."

"OK. Take it slow, but keep contact while I come to you," radioed Jason.

Within minutes Jason pulled alongside. "You guys are great. The other boats will fall in behind us. We're now going to be very patient because we need Z-28 to split off and go on a fishing trip of her own. She'll be fishing for two. We can't try a capture with other members of her family around. We didn't know she had a new young one. Looks like less than six weeks old."

Jason took the lead as we followed the little family group slowly south. He gave them some distance but kept a close watch with binoculars. He expected this mini pod with a young one would stay in the marsh and not head out into the open ocean. Luck was with us when Z-28 left the others and turned into a moderate-sized creek.

Jason radioed. "She's going up this stream on a fishing trip. Let's set up just a little ways into this creek and nab her when she comes back looking for her pod. One boat follow her in and see if you can carefully encourage her to turn around. The water here looks about six feet but it'll be going down as the tide begins to move out faster. Looks like a great place to make our move. She's being very helpful."

"We'll stay behind you," said Papa Joe as he edged our boat to the mud bank of the creek. "Throw the anchor out Jack and tighten us in."

We all waited. Patience in fishing applied equally to rescues. Z-28 was more interested in the fish in the stream than she was in her entourage and took her time. She was smart and over many years had learned humans were not a threat unless they were moving in a fast boat. Fishing must have been good because it was an hour before she turned downstream and started toward the boats blocking the stream.

The radio spoke. "She's turning back. Following a school of minnows."

Jason stood in the front of his boat and lowered the net into the water. He used a long pole to push it up either side of the creek. The other boats were in front of him, hugging the bank. "We're ready. Throw a few apples out to attract her attention."

"I see her!"

I had a good view of the net.

Z-28 slowed her swim when she came around a big S turn and sensed the boats. She had good eyesight up to only 150 feet, but echolocation told her exactly where they were. Four of the team pulled their wet suits up and slipped on protective shoes, then positioned themselves inside the net but along both banks. Z-28 moved comfortably toward the gaggle of boats. She saw the team's apples near the net and swam toward one. The team moved to the center of the stream and circled the net behind her. They all waited a moment while she went for another apple.

"OK. Close in a little. Everybody ready?" asked Jason. All thumbs were up.

I touched the red video button.

"She's nosing the net and getting upset. Let's take her!"

With the first human touch, she gave a powerful flip of her tail flukes, narrowly missing one of the men, and dove to the bottom. They held on and went under with her. After some breathless, heart-thumping moments, they slowly lifted her to the surface so all could get a breath.

The captors edged her close to Jason's boat. In their loose grasp, she calmed a little.

The veterinarian took charge. He examined the heavy polymer fishing line wrapped around her dorsal fin and knew it had to come off. He clipped both sides near the front, which was dangerously close to an artery, and pulled it slowly out one side.

"It's off," the vet shouted. He decided precautionary antibiotics were needed and gave her an injection near the wound.

"Can I take another minute for a blood sample?" he asked Jason.

"Go for it. I think she's good." He moved quickly and confidently, but it took a minute to get a single full vial of her blood.

While they waited, the vet repeated what everyone already knew. "The analysis of dolphin blood is a good way to find out if there are any toxins in this marsh food chain. Since they're at the top of the chain, anything bad below them will end up in their blood."

"Her blood will help us with a lot of our future research," Jason said.

"It's almost like she knows we're trying to help her," I observed. It turned out to be a nice bit of audio for my video.

Jason got everyone's attention, then he ordered, "Let's get the net out of the way before we do the release. Take it into the boat on the right."

"OK. We're good to go. Let's get out of her way." The boats blocking the creek drifted to the bank. The men released their tight hold.

Z-28 swam free. With a firm stroke of her tail she passed Jason's boat and headed to the marsh river and her family. "She has a great story to tell her family," I said just before I stopped the video.

They were done. A cheer went up from the five team boats. Full-grown, burly men raised their arms in the air and whooped with joy at the success of the rescue.

It couldn't have taken more than four minutes. It was one dolphin out of hundreds, maybe thousands, but this act drew a connection, human to dolphin, man to fellow mammal, far beyond this one act of kindness.

I captured it all! I hoped the world would see this beautiful creature and the kindness of the men who did the rescue. And, of course, my friends. *Maybe viral on Instagram,* I thought.

One of the NOAA crew cautioned me about the video. "It's OK to show others the process, but don't let people know where we are. Too much attention from people who don't think carefully enough could make life difficult for Z-28 and the rest of her pod."

"I understand. No map, no directions," I readily agreed. "I like the idea of keeping it a secret. I also don't want many people to know where our campsite's located. We might not be able to use it next time. And we've seen what unthinking people can do to the wild-life out here. Did the pics we took of the hatchling kill get to you?"

"No. I didn't keep up well yesterday. Too much prep going on. I'm sure someone has them. You guys seem to have a clear back door to our Coastal Division staff."

I handed Jason a small zip-lock bag we had in-scribed with date and time. "We have a specimen we hope you get to the right person. It's a hatchling we found dead on the sandbar south of here last night. Looks like a dog owner let his pet run free, and this dead little guy is the result. With a little investigation you might be able to identify the owner. We think it's the builder of the marsh kitchen we ran into yesterday. A size-10 flip-flop print near this tiny carcass seems to match what we saw him wearing yesterday and is captured in the video of our conversation. He likes his big German Shepherd to run free on these sandbars. I'd love him to develop the same kind of love for the creatures who depend on this environment. Maybe he could own up to the damage his dog did." *Whew, now I was starting to lecture or maybe even preach.*

"You guys are fierce advocates," Jason said. "I love it. I'll make sure our enforcement people follow your evidence. This is a great environment, and we want people to use it smartly."

"When the investigator gets started, I'd like to help him go in the right direction," I offered.

"I'll make sure the investigator gets in touch with you, and they'll appreciate all the help you can give them. It takes all of us to protect this place," he added.

"Little Tybee's officially a heritage island which means we, the Department of Natural Resources, can put up all kinds of signs and require users to get a permit to be here. We don't want to do that, but some people seem to be overusing the privilege. This can be a free space for humans, but first of all it has to be a free space for the wildlife."

Papa Joe, feeling a little defensive of his community, spoke up, "For years local people who come here have carted away their stuff plus the stuff left behind by a few unthinking tourists. We like the partnership with DNR, but we don't want a lot of signs."

"It takes all of us working together," agreed Jason. "You guys are really our messengers. End of lecture," he added with satisfaction written all over his face. He pulled his sleek NOAA boat away, waving his hat as the boat disappeared around the end of the island.

With little food, our batteries almost dead, and gas nearly gone, the next task for Papa Joe and me was to get back to his home in one piece.

Chapter 17

Back at our campsite, I sat on a log reviewing the rescue in my head. "Papa Joe, those rescuers did an amazing thing."

"I'd heard about rescues, but that was a first for me. Just think about all the knowledge and coordination it took to make those four minutes happen. Lots of experience showed up—three states, the federal government, and a private company! Everybody worked together to save Mrs. Z-28."

"She didn't know where we came from," I observed, "but from the way she relaxed in the workers' arms, I think she knew we were on her side. I wonder if she was able to tell her pod what happened."

"Dolphins do talk, but they may not be strong story-tellers like we humans. They stick to the facts. Our challenge is to get those facts into a story people can see and feel. Feelings are what make us humans take action."

"Speaking of which," I said as I reached for my phone, "I have to get this story out to the world. I think a lot of people will get the right feeling from seeing it. Posting on Instagram is fine for my friends, but if I want others to see it, I think I need to put it up on YouTube using the hashtag, '*Dolphin Rescue and Georgia coast*.' Then I'll send a link to the people who know what we've been doing."

While I started tapping on my phone, Papa Joe seemed to need something to calm him down a notch.

He put on his waders and walked into the water with his fishing rod. The spot at the end of the island was still the perfect fishing hole. As he fished, I could hear him say to himself, *"Billy and Willard will love to celebrate the adventures I've had with Jack this week and get to know him in person. I think I'll ask them to a fish fry tonight."*

I interrupted his musing. "All done," I said. "The world will soon be able to see Z-28 and her rescuers. It could use some edits, maybe some dramatic music, some voice-over commentary. Most people like the raw video. Hmm, maybe there could be a shorter version, but I think this will keep viewer attention for four minutes."

"Where did you send the link?" Papa Joe asked.

"The video's now on the beach at Hilton Head and the Emerald Coast of Florida. Jason can see it when he gets back to his dock, and Jane Olmstead and her NOAA team have it. She probably has some people who can polish it. I also sent it to Billy, Willard, Mom and Dad. Like I said, the world can now see what we did here."

"Jack, call your mom. I'm sure she'd love to celebrate this moment with you. She'll probably like a two-way phone call better than a text." Papa Joe proudly suggested.

"I'll do it."

Mom answered on the first ring. "How are my two wilderness adventurers doing?"

"We're riding high." I answered. "We just got back to the campsite after helping the rescuers get the fishing line off Z-28. She swam away free—no more polymer fishing line."

"That's more than I can imagine. Amazing! Awesome!"

"I even got most of the action on video from close

up so you and the world can see what these guys did today."

"The world?"

"Yeah! I just posted it on YouTube. I sent you a link, and if you go there, you can be right in the middle of the action."

"Wow! That IS amazing. When did I miss you becoming a videographer? I'm impressed, and I think the world's also going to be impressed. I'll look at it as soon as we get off."

"Mom, you won't believe I'm saying this but," I hesitated, then rushed on, "thanks for sending me down here to be with Papa Joe. It's been great, and he's great. I love this place! But right now I gotta go. We're packing up the camp and headed home. We've got to get everything we brought out of here. The tide's already started to turn. We gotta get going! And we're both running out of battery. Bye Mom."

I didn't really hear the rest of the conversation as my mind was already thinking about steering the boat home.

"Your dad will be back in from southwest Georgia, and maybe we can both get on the line with you," Mom continued.

"Ok. Talk later."

"Do be careful," I heard her say as I clicked off. Papa Joe had already started packing.

As he put away his fishing gear, I heard him saying to himself, "What effect might Jack's video have if some state decision makers see it? Maybe someone in DNR will show the video to the governor and see the work of his specialists. There are still a lot of coastal issues the current governor and legislators need to know about."

I voiced similar thoughts. "Maybe we could take the video to the governor at Little People's Day."

"I don't think governors do that anymore. Too little control over who might show up for the media attention and embarrass the governor. It's a good thought though. There are a lot of new organizations trying to protect the coast, and maybe their members would like to see this. They know how to get in front of the governor. Maybe even the local legislators. I'm sure Billy and Willard keep up with them, and they can usually get anyone's attention when they get going."

"It's a little like what you, Billy, and Willard did," I observed.

"Well, I do see the connection, but it's a very different world with social media. Things come on my computer I don't even ask for. I don't really understand it. But I sure am glad young folks like you understand it and can use it for good. We see enough of the bad that comes from it."

I smiled a little, realizing social media, like the marsh, has its dark sides.

Papa Joe broke into my thoughts, "We probably need to get serious about going home. There isn't much ice on those fish I just caught, and our other supplies are gone. Let's pack and scrub the site. I hope there's enough gas to get us back to my dock. We'll need to go through the Cut."

"How about we ask Billy and Willard to come to your place this evening to have grilled fish? We have enough fish, and maybe we could grab some more oysters on our way back. It'd be great to meet your friends. Call them on *your* phone. My video and call to mom took all my battery power. Good thing we brought two phones."

Papa Joe was pleased and smiled as he punched Billy's number. He expected Billy would be able to pass the invitation on to Willard and his wife. This was going to be a fun way to end the day. I could hear his conversation.

"This is Billy. Good to hear from you. I expect you were there for the rescue. I'll want to hear all the details, but right now I'm driving."

"We're headed back, and we wanted to ..."

Billy interrupted, "My wife and I are headed to the hospital in Savannah. Her cold or flu turned out to be Covid, and the doctor told us to get to the hospital so they can monitor her oxygen levels. They may want to give her some of that new anti-viral medicine. We just pulled out of our driveway. Willard knows, and he's meeting us there."

"Oh my! I'm so sorry. What more did the doctor say?"

"She does seem a little out of breath and has some fever. We've both been vaccinated and boosted, but the doctor wants to keep close tabs."

"That makes sense. Good she's getting the attention she needs. We're starting back home in a couple of minutes. I'll check in on you this evening," Papa Joe said, ending the call.

Chapter 18

The packing and cleaning went quickly. Everything had to go. We threw the sleeping bags, tents, and pads into the bow of the boat. The pots and pans, cooler, crab traps, and garbage bag were in the middle of the boat, which was as low in the water as the first day of the adventure. We ate the last of the bread and peanut butter and were soon on board heading north on the Slough. I was at the helm.

Along the way we caught one last view of a Great Blue Heron poised to strike something for dinner. Approaching the Cut, I could see the ebbing tide was moving quickly but the water was still slightly above the creek's banks and getting through shouldn't be a problem.

"Let's stop at this oyster reef and pick up a new batch before we go through," Papa Joe suggested.

I gave the motor a little extra gas, and the boat slid over the submerged oysters. The bow came to rest on the exposed bed. I could hear the oysters scraping the flat aluminum bottom. To save on gas, I cut the motor. I stepped into the water with my oyster boots while Papa Joe was pulling his on. When he stepped onto the oysters, the boat started to float and drift into the moving water.

"Jack, you push, and I'll pull it a little further up the reef. Hold the boat at the stern while I gather the oysters. I want to walk this oyster reef just a little and see if I can scare out the Clapper Rails we heard here

before. Oh, and throw me that mesh bag for the oysters. It's under the stern seat."

"Be careful," I warned as I tossed the bag toward
Papa Joe's outstretched hand. It didn't quite get there.

He stretched to catch it. Trying to balance against
a fall forward, he corrected the forward lunge by lean-
ing back. Too far. His feet slipped on the wet oysters
under him, and he went down full force on his back,
banging his head on a clump of large oysters on the
reef.

He was stunned, but he could still think. *After all
these years how could I make such a stupid mistake?
I warned Jack, Sharon, and all the people on my ECO
Tour for years about the danger of the oyster beds. I
know they can cut like razors. With all my experience
in the marsh, how could this possibly happen to me?*

I jumped to his side on the reef. I saw the pain in
his face, but his eyes were open. How bad could it be?
Then I saw the blood running down the right forearm
and coating the oysters below. It looked like an oyster
had found an artery or a vein. I looked up. I could see
urban Tybee just over the top of the marsh grass. A
marsh and a shallow creek separated us from civilization. It was a short distance but a long way to medical
care.

"Papa Joe, we have a problem. You're bleeding a
lot," I said trying to keep my voice steady.

He mumbled something about the first aid kit,
and that got me moving. I pulled the boat up further
on the reef to keep it from floating away and reached
under the stern seat for the kit. *My mind flashed back
to the church basement and the Boy Scout leader di-
recting us, "The first thing you do is stop the flow of
the blood." "How do you do that?" Toni had asked. "Cut
off the flow of the blood above the wound. You can use
a strap, your belt, even a makeshift tourniquet with a*

stick and long cloth. Wrap it around the limb and twist it with the stick."

There was a small strap in the kit that could be used for a tourniquet. I had never used it before but recalled the demonstration. I grabbed a screwdriver from the tool box, tied the strap loosely above the wound and twisted it tight with the screwdriver. The blood slowed a little. One more turn. A few drops continued to come, but most of the flow had stopped. Some blood flow to the arm was needed.

"Papa Joe, hold this tourniquet in place with your left hand. Can you sit up a little? I want to check for wounds on your back."

Oyster shells protruded from his back, and I knew we were in big trouble. Papa Joe had told me about the danger of oyster beds, but it was still surprising how much damage the fall had done. He was really cut up, stunned and disoriented.

"We're going to need help," Papa Joe answered through clenched teeth. "Use my phone. It's in the bow."

I grabbed the phone. It was down to 10% power. I found Willard's number. No time for a long explanation.

"Willard, this is Jack. We're in trouble. Papa Joe fell on an oyster reef and is badly cut. We need to get him to a hospital."

"Oh Lord no! Where are you? Are you near the Cut? Do you think you can get him in the boat?" Willard spoke quickly, not waiting for an answer. "I'm turning around and heading back to Tybee. If you can get him in the boat, I can get a Tybee ambulance to meet you at the boat ramp on the Back River. That's probably the quickest route to help. We could call the Coast Guard, but that'll take more time. Their large boats will have to go around the south end of the island, and with the ebbing tide they may not be able to get through."

"If he can help a little, I think I can get him into the boat. We're at the beginning of the Cut, and I think there's still enough water to get through. We probably don't have enough gas to go south and around the sandbars if the Cut is too low."

I looked at Papa Joe's graying face "And we don't have much time. The Cut is our best option."

I knew it was our *only* option.

"OK. That's the plan for now," Willard said.

"One other thing. Neither of us have much battery on our phones. If you don't hear from me or see our boat very soon, get a different rescue started. We'll need a new plan," I warned.

"Roger that. Out"

I pushed the boat a little more into the water and pulled it as close to Papa Joe's side as I could. Squatting down, I helped him come to a sitting position. The punctures on his back were shocking, but none of the wounds were bleeding like the arm. Some oysters were embedded in his skin and the back of his head. "Crook your right arm to hold the tourniquet and put your left arm over my shoulder. We'll lift together and get you over the edge of the boat."

I got into a position so I could lift with my legs.

"OK, on three, I'll lift, and you push up with your legs. Ready. One, two, three."

Together we rose up just enough to get him over the gunnel. Papa Joe fell into the bow on top of the sleeping bags and tents. They gave just a little cushion. He cried out from the pain and shock. The oysters went deeper into his back.

After a moment he did manage to say, "Jack, pour the antiseptic from the first-aid kit over my back." We both feared the bacteria that usually sticks to oyster shells.

I pulled a little bottle of ancient Iodine from the old kit and some Tylenol. "This is really going to hurt."

After he took three of the tablets, Papa Joe clenched his teeth and nodded to show he was ready for the sting. I poured, and Papa Joe stifled a scream between his clenched teeth and his tightly-pressed lips. The pain meds were probably of little help, but doing something was better than feeling helpless.

With this done, Papa Joe leaned back on his side on the sleeping bags in the bow and got ready for the motion of the boat.

Worried about pushing off the reef, I lightened the load by throwing the crab traps, the anchor, the cast net, the cooler with the fish, and the empty gas tank out of the boat. Then, with all my might, I managed to push the bow partly off the oyster reef. I jumped into the stern which had just enough water under it to cover the propeller. With my weight now in the back of the boat, it was almost floating. I used an oar to push the boat free of the reef. Questions raced through my mind. Would the engine start? Would there be enough gas? Would there still be enough water in the Cut?

I remembered Papa Joe explaining the decompression feature of the Yamaha 15 that was supposed to make pull-starting easier. It wasn't easier. It was hard enough to make me swear. I took two deep breaths to calm myself down and made sure I did all the steps right. I put the ignition key to on. No choke with a warm engine. Gear select to neutral. Throttle turned to start. I pulled the starter cord out a little to engage it and then gave it a long pull. There was a quiet thump thump engine sound, but no start. Once, twice. No go! Again a long pull. No start.

A sharp pain shot up my right arm from the full-on effort. "Damn! Start dammit!" I pulled with all my might. More thump thump, still no start. I counted to ten and thought *I don't usually do this but, Oh God help me! It needs to start now and run full on to get Papa Joe to help.* I glanced at Papa Joe and saw pain written across his face, looking grayer and weaker. Barely hanging on.

Don't panic. With my arm aching, I braced my foot on the bench seat and pulled, throwing my full weight back as I focused every last bit of strength on the starter cord. I fell back onto the middle seat and ignored the bruising when the engine fired then smoothly ran to idle. I backed away from the reef, switched gears, and headed into the narrowing Cut. If the Clapper Rails clapped, I didn't hear them.

The water in the creek was now significantly below the mud banks. *We've gotta get through here. No time. No gas to go around.*

Now that we were moving, I needed all my new-found boating skills to keep from getting stuck. I pulled the motor up and locked it in place, so the propeller turned just below the water line and out of the mud. I took the curves fast staying on the inside where the current cut a little deeper channel. I read the movement of the water around each sharp curve. A quick glance at Papa Joe. His eyes were closed, and his hands held tight across his chest. It was moving up and down.

I felt the muddy bottom slow the boat several times, so I gave the engine more gas when it was needed to get through a shallow spot. The propeller churned up the mud on the bottom, but the boat kept moving. I was scared out of my wits, but my mind was intensely focused on the water. Fear was a good motivator.

Time moved slowly. *Where did all these extra turns come from? Come on! One more turn and I'm through the Cut.* At the entrance of the Back River I

slowed to pick the deepest channel through the sandbars that shifted with the daily tides. I watched the
ripples on the surface of the water and steered the
boat to the deeper water. When I reached the edge of
the Back River, I dropped the engine shaft and twisted
to full throttle.

The engine emitted a high-pitched whine at max-
imum power and pushed us toward help. Now I felt
the burning sting of the big scrape on my own arm.
It must have happened falling back getting the motor
started. Blood was running down my arm, but I told
myself to ignore it. I looked again at Papa Joe.

My grandpa was helpless in a way I had not seen
before. Lying still in the bow of the boat, wet, bleeding,
and oyster-cut, I saw deep lines in his face. Then Papa
Joe looked straight at me. With that look I saw he was
now totally relying on me. This was new. No one had
ever relied on me like this before. Papa Joe closed his
eyes, but I could see his chest still rising and falling.

Looking up, I saw the flashing lights of the ambulance at the boat ramp across the river. It looked
far away, but in only moments I was slowing near the
ramp. Willard and the attendants standing in the water grabbed hold of the boat to pull it up the ramp
toward the open back door of the ambulance.

"Here's the biggest threat. I pointed to Papa Joe's
right arm. "Did I do this right?"

The EMTs checked. "Looks good for now. We'll
put some pressure on the wound and get him hooked
to some fluids. The monitors will tell us more."

The two EMTs, Willard, and I carefully lifted Papa
Joe out of the boat and put him in a sitting position
on the stretcher to keep pressure off his back. "On my
count," one of the EMTs directed. "One, two, three."
We lifted the stretcher into the vehicle, and I jumped
in. I made it clear I was riding to the hospital with Papa

Joe.

"I'll get someone to take care of the boat and meet you at the hospital," Willard offered with a lot of relief in his voice.

The sirens screamed as we sped over the causeway to Savannah. While the EMTs worked quickly and carefully on Papa Joe's wounds, I knew there was a call I had to make. There was just one bar left on Papa Joe's phone.

"Mom, there's been an accident. I'm fine, but Papa Joe was cut when he fell on an oyster reef. We're in an ambulance headed for the hospital in Savannah. The EMTs say he's going to need surgery, and they're treating him for shock, but they say he's going to be OK," I pushed my explanation rapidly into the phone, trying to sound confident so as not to frighten my mom.

"Oh no!"

"But I'm OK, Mom, and Papa Joe will be too."

"I'm on my way, Jack. Hang in there. I love you."

"I love you too, Mom," I whispered as the phone went silent.

Jack

Chapter 19

In the dimmed light of the hospital room, I sat by my grandpa's bed. Alone.

I could hear the hushed voices in the hall, loud pages from the nursing desk, the roll of the wheeled dinner carts. But my attention was on Papa Joe. I couldn't take my eyes off of him. The rise and fall of his slow breathing.

"Is that you, Jack?" the raspy voice came from the bed.

"Yes sir, it's me," I answered, moving closer.

I explained the silent room. "Just a few minutes ago there was a crowd here for the report from the surgeon, but they've scattered for the moment. Mom is headed to the airport to pick Dad up."

"Give me the bad news from the doctor," Papa Joe growled.

"It's good news! You're gonna live many more years. The hit on the reef rattled your brain some so it'll take a few weeks for it to fully recover. All the oyster holes are cleaned out, sterilized and sewn up. They had to give you three pints of blood. Despite my tourniquet you lost a lot from your arm. You'll want to take some pain killers and move slowly for a while. But the best news is," I paused for effect, "there's no reason we can't get back out in the marsh when my school lets out this summer."

I let that statement sink in for a minute.

When there was no immediate reply, I asked,

"Shall I call the nurse to check on you? They told me to do that."

"Let's wait a minute. My brain is slowly unscrambling. I bet there'll be plenty of time for everybody to tell me what I should or shouldn't be doing. We both know how that is. Let's leave it with the two of us for a little longer. I've loved it being just the two of us this week."

"I hope you're looking forward to being around a lot longer so we can have more adventures."

"I certainly am! Maybe with a little less excitement. I'm sure glad I got to know you and want to see where you're going in the future."

"I think I've seen some places this last week where I'd like to spend more time. That campsite, for one. Fishing, for another. What about you—what will you be doing?"

As Papa Joe reached for a cup of water near the bed, I jumped up to help. After a few sips and a little cough, he said, "That's a good question. I'm sure you're going to hear that a lot, and I'm glad you're tossing it back at me. No matter our age we all ought to be asked that question."

"I'm ready to start looking for my answer," I said. "Our days in the marsh showed me there are a lot of mysteries to learn about and experiences out there."

"I want to watch you do that. My options are a little narrower. I'm probably not going to be a PhD biologist, but I'd like to make more use of what I know about this beautiful coast. Maybe some of my experience could be helpful in this rapidly changing world of ours."

"You've got plenty of time, Papa Joe. You could start by sharing the story of saving Little Tybee. I bet many people don't know what you and your friends did."

"Kerr-McGee did get stopped in their tracks, but the governor didn't listen to just us boys. There were a whole lot of people who helped Governor Lester Maddox understand what was good for the coast and the state. Those smart young scientists, ladies' garden clubs, hunters, and fishermen. It took a lot of little people to get behind an idea and speak up like we did."

"So, that's the end of the story?"

"No. The legislator I told you about said there needed to be a law protecting the marshlands. He was a very focused and determined guy. It took two years to get support from all over the state before enough legislators voted to pass the bill. Old Lester scratched his head for a little while, then finally signed it into law. It's the law today. And later Governor Miller found some money to buy Little Tybee from Kerr-McGee."

"So **that's** the end of the story, right?"

"I wish it was, but the coast is never saved forever. There are always people looking for new ways to get what they want. Somebody always wants to live right on the edge of the sea and doesn't care what or who that's going to affect. Then there are natural challenges like sea-level rise which will need different solutions. You and your friends will have to deal with those problems."

"Wait! Wait just a minute. You don't get to opt out. If I and my friends get going on this, you and your friends damn well better be there with us!" I said, blushing at my language and vehemence.

Papa Joe chuckled. "OK. You're probably right. I've been moping around in my lonely house for too long and need some young people to give me inspiration and a push out the door. You've given me that this week."

"And I also need to tell you what was on the front page of the *Savannah Morning Post* this morning," I said gleefully. "They must have a reporter who follows social media to see if there are stories they need to cover. It's not a big picture, but the hummock kitchen is on the front page. There is a quote from a DNR spokesperson saying the Coastal Division is planning to remove those facilities. Our little nudge might have made a difference."

"I told you Billy would know how to gig the officials."

"Hey, Papa Joe, you could come to Atlanta and stay with us when the legislature gets going. I'm sure those environmental groups you mentioned are working on laws to protect the coast, and they could use some help from old guys who know a lot. I bet some of those 'Suits' under the Capitol's gold dome might listen to a tour boat captain who knows the marshlands up close and personal," I said tilting my head towards Papa Joe's bandaged wounds.

"Well, I'll think about it," Papa Joe replied and closed his eyes.

I sat quietly by the hospital bed.

Smiling to myself, I called up my YouTube video and reviewed the rescue.

Acknowledgements

For me, it takes a host of supporters to brave the challenges of writing. Like all writers, I put the words on the paper in solitude but within hours, or sometimes days, I like to hear what someone else thinks. My wife, Livija (Riki), bears the brunt of giving the first reaction to my "perfect" words. Without her careful mind for words, my ideas and dramas would not be clear to others. Her creative strength is on display in her first book of poetry published this year by Finishing Line Press, <u>Ize's Daughter</u>.

Every writer should have a small group that convenes regularly to critique and encourage production. I am proud to be part of an all-women's writing group that listens, hears, questions, edits, and on occasion, applauds at the right time. Our regular members are: Debbie Miller, Carla Schissel, Riki Bolster, Kate Sitter. We lost one of our lovely lyrical writers last year, Kaaren Nowicki.

Writers need a cheering squad. Two friends stand out. Thanks to Robert Searfoss for his unending enthusiasm, his technical knowledge of the compression cycle of an outboard motor, and the fright he saw in Papa Joe's eyes. And to my friend, Dr. Fred Marland, who more than 50 years ago brought science to bear on the political process in unrestrained advocacy for the natural environment of Georgia's coast. I am very pleased he thinks me "coach-able." You can find him disguised in this novel.

Two teens, who I think will help save us from ourselves in the next generation, made meaningful contributions to Jack's language. My granddaughter Zahna Taylor, wanted to like Jack. She helped me see Jack needed to tell his own story. Catarina Boers carefully read every single word and helped Jack speak the language of his generation.

My friend and artist, Paul Buechele, did the illustrations which helped set the scene for the story. A high school artist, Elizavata Kalacheva, with a long creative career ahead, caught the mood of the wild spring break adventure for the painting on the cover. My artist daughter, Lillian, in her painting on the back cover, captures what my wife and I miss most about our Tybee years. Thank you to my son, Nathan, who was always available with his artistic and technical assistance.

Many thanks and much admiration to the founders and editors of Maudlin Pond Press. With dedication and fortitude they have breached the fortifications of the publishing industry and made opportunities for first time writers to see our work in published form. Thanks especially to Cathy Sakas for believing in this project and providing the technical support to get it across the finish line.

My wife, Riki, holds me close and keeps me sane when the world doesn't go as I would plan. Without sanity there is no literature.

www.ingramcontent.com/pod-product-compliance
Lightning Source LLC
Chambersburg PA
CBHW010602310726
48969CB00009B/2532